OFFICE *Hate*

#1 *New York Times* Bestselling Author

RACHEL VAN DYKEN

Office Hate
by Rachel Van Dyken

OFFICE HATE

ISBN: 978-1-946061-85-0
Cover Design by Letitia Hasser, r.b.a. Designs
Editing by Kay Springsteen
Formatting & Editing by Jill Sava, Love Affair With Fiction

DEDICATION

To *Tia* (aka *Michelle*) and *Jill*,
this book would NEVER have even happened without you,
and to *Carson*
for being the best Max a girl could ever ask for!

RIGHT *Away*

I am so thrilled to bring this original song to you!
I love what Indi Anderson & Kyler Daron created.

I was listening to Indi's newest music, and this one really resonated with me for Office Hate.
Mark and Olivia are in this constant battle, and this just brought forth their sexiness and rivalry. After the games are over and the doors are closed, they're behind the scenes, unable to keep their hands off each other!

Enjoy this original song for Office Hate!
Listen to Right Away on my website:
www.rachelvandykenauthor.com

PROLOGUE

Olivia

1 year previous

"Think of it this way. We graduate college in less than four hours, you're going to end up becoming this badass marketing strategist, and you'll never have to see him again." Amelia patted me on the head while I glared at my nemesis across the huge gym of our private university.

Mark Huxley.

The bane of my existence since freshman year when I went to a frat party, and he gave me a bloody nose.

It wasn't his fault.

I mean, not really.

If I really wanted to dissect it, I was partially to blame. I'd had a little too much wine, tripped over my own shoe, and he just happened to be coming out of the stupid bathroom with one of his many fans on his arm and lipstick all over his face.

He rammed right into me, spilling his beer all over my brand new Jordans, and then tripped over the girl still clinging to him, sending his elbow flying across my face as he tried to hold her up while I went sailing to the floor.

I remember blinking up at him and waiting for him to offer his hand. Instead, the girl on his arm stepped *over* me with her giant heels, and he chased after her like she had a magic snatch.

I had to recover all on my own.

And that wasn't the first time we'd had a run-in.

We'd carried the same major, business with a minor in marketing.

So all the same classes, save one, archery, which let's be honest, he and I and archery would have ended up in complete and total bloodshed.

"Seriously, though." I crossed my arms and glared. "Why does everyone love him so much?"

Amelia gulped and tucked her short black hair behind her ear as the president of the university droned on and on about our guest speaker.

"He's hot," she finally blurted. "Sorry, I mean I have eyes, and his are so blue…"

It irritated me that God had gifted him with a perfect body to boot. I mean, if he was going to have that nice of a face, could he have at least had bacne? Weird toes? A thripple?

As if sensing my hateful thoughts, he and his friend Ryker both turned in my direction. Ryker smiled. He was almost as bad as Mark with his curly blond hair and green eyes.

He elbowed Mark, who chose that moment to smirk and then wink at me. The absolute nerve of that jackass!

"Sit. Down." Amelia grabbed my arm. "You can't take

him. He's twice your size, and you'll just end up with another bloody nose."

Wait, was I actually getting up?

He made me insane!

I was losing my mind during my own graduation ceremony!

I huffed, sitting back in my chair, ready to give him the finger when he finger waved at me like we were best friends, and yup, I was going to shove those fingers down his throat and yell something like, "Die, bitch, die!"

"...CEO of Emory Enterprises, Max Emory!" The dean was really hard up on this guy; he looked ready to pass out as he shook this Max guy's hand and then gave him the microphone.

Max was really attractive for someone in his thirties. Huh, CEO before forty, he was living my best life.

I wanted that.

I deserved that.

I'd worked hard for that.

I chewed my lower lip, all memory of Mark forgotten as I zeroed in on whatever life advice this speaker was going to give us.

"It's a pleasure to be here." His toothy grin had several girls in the audience fanning themselves and making sighing noises.

Disgusting.

Give me the details on how to be a CEO, damn it!

Gimme!

"When they asked me to give the commencement speech, I knew that it had to be something special, something that you'd think back on, something..." He paused for obvious dramatic effect. "...that you would take with you for the rest of your life." He chuckled. "And then I remembered my commencement ceremony, or lack thereof. The drunkenness, the nakedness, the sheer boredom of sitting on my ass for hours while some old guy told me how to live my life…"

As though cued up, people laughed.

"So I'm not going to bore you with inspiration on how making your bed means you'll make better choices, or that if you work super hard you're going to become a millionaire like me."

More laughter.

"I wrote a book on success, and what I've learned is that a lot of it is luck. Yes, it's hard work, but at the end of the day… you need to remember to never sign anything without reading it first. Always have a wingman, even if it's a gecko. Never, and I do mean never, do a reality show where you're the bachelor, and you have psychotic women thrusting their bosoms in your face, and above all…when you're given a chance to do something epic—you take it. Feel me?" He laughed and then cracked his knuckles and went on. "You probably understood none of that, and that's kind of the point, isn't it? Half of you are listening. Half are starving. Some didn't even show up, so what's the point. Am I right?"

Who the hell was this guy?

"Some might remember the gecko part or the stay true to yourself part or the not signing anything part, and all of those are good life lessons, but I'm going to drop one major one, and then I'm going to drop the mic and let you guys get out of here so you can binge drink one last time before life fucks you." Gasps were heard all over the stadium. "Nobody, and I do mean nobody, is owed anything. If you want it, you take it. That's it, that's my advice. If you want something, you take it, you work hard for it, and you own up to your own failures when eventually you don't get what you want because ninety-nine percent of you will be working at some random job in the next year, with student loan debt up your ass, and wondering what's so bad about living with your parents. But the one percent of people in here who want to tell me where to shove it, I look forward to seeing you change the world. The ninety-nine percent left, I suggest you learn how to coupon, so you can survive on something more than ramen every day. Welcome to adulthood." He grinned. "I wish I was kidding. Also, I'm using this time to announce that Emory Enterprises is seeking interns for this summer. Whoever does the best—" he hesitated and then "—job will be offered a lucrative signing bonus, company car, and full salary in the best place where they fit in my company. Good luck to you all. And remember…life doesn't owe you shit."

He literally dropped the mic, walked off the stage, head held high.

And I'd never been more traumatized or driven to not be the fry girl. I would not be moving back in with my parents! They collected dolls! The creepy porcelain ones that look like they're plotting your death. On top of that, both my mom and dad were exhibitionists! They've been arrested multiple times in the Walmart parking lot, and let me tell you, there's nothing more traumatic than bailing your parents out of jail while they suck face. Even the police, who have literally seen it all, weren't making eye contact with me.

That internship was mine.

And as if Mark could hear the challenge from the universe, I turned to see him lock eyes with me, one eyebrow quirked upward as if to say game on.

"Game on, you psycho," I growled.

"Why are you repeating that over and over again?" Amelia whispered.

"Sorry," I snapped, then looked back over to Mark only to see him still staring directly at me, his eyes mercilessly raking over my body as if measuring me up.

"He's dead to me."

"You're scaring me." Amelia laughed uncomfortably.

"Good." I nodded my head, then leaned back in my chair and huffed. "Good."

CHAPTER *One*

Mark

Present day

I'd been convinced that I was the perfect candidate for Emory Enterprises, only to find out that the waitlist had been hundreds of applicants long. So, for the next year, what did I do?

Exactly what he said I would.

The only job I could get was working at a car dealership as a fucking receptionist—yes, a male receptionist. Times are changing, okay? Lay the fuck off!

Part of my job entailed greeting customers and then calling over the loudspeaker for certain sales managers to come forward and meet their clients. Then I was privy to all the long waits with financial, where the salesman went back and bullshitted for at least an hour before coming back and "making the deal of a century" for their client.

Now, here's the thing. I know some dealerships are awesome on customer service, and I have nothing against car salesmen; some of them make bank and really care about getting people into the right car.

But I wasn't at that sort of dealership.

I was at Fancy Fred's.

Fancy. Fred's.

And across the street, my nemesis stood, at the Audi dealership, dressed in black every single day, wearing perfect makeup, heels, and somehow staring daggers at me across the parking lot as if she had won.

Which, technically, in the job department she had.

When I graduated with my business degree, I wasn't really picturing the guy walking by me with day-old coffee in his mug and a tie with eyesores on it, as if his own clothing even knew it was rough waters over at Fancy Fred's.

I'd imagined skyscrapers.

Headhunting.

City life.

I had imagined driving that Audi not watching someone else sell them.

At least I wasn't living with my parents. I guess in that area, I won, where Olivia lost. I heard through Ryker, who heard through his new girlfriend Amelia that Olivia hadn't been able to afford her expensive apartment and, to save money, had moved home.

Which seemed odd since she had the better job out of the two of us, and I was the one living with a roommate.

Whatever. Why the hell was I so fixated on her anyway?

She'd always looked down her nose at me. Always. And in order to protect myself, I baited her, and man, did she take the bait, every single time.

Which entertained me to no end.

Hell, I made out with girls in front of her just to see that blush burn across her cheeks and her indignant huff.

Fuck, I was getting hard just thinking about it.

Nothing better than an erection at Fancy Fred's while listening to soft adult rock for the last seven hours.

If a criminal decided to come in and take hostages, I'd probably be the first volunteer.

"Hey!" Fred—you guessed it, our owner—stepped out of his office, his thick white hair in disarray while his black glasses hung low on his nose. He was pulling out a hanky and blowing into it, then shoving it back into his black trousers before tucking in his matching black button-down as if he'd just had a quickie with the lady from finance.

Was he flushed?

I cleared my throat. "Sir, nice to see you today."

"Yeaaahhhhhh…" He leaned so far over the receptionist desk that I shoved my rolling chair back. Huh, maybe if I spun in it, I'd pass out and wouldn't have to have this conversation. "I'm gonna have to let you go, squirt."

Oh yeah, and he called me squirt like I was ten, not twenty-two.

Wait, what?

"Excuse me?" My eyes narrowed. "I don't think I understand."

"You…" he said slowly as he pointed his heavily jeweled hand in my direction, "are being let go."

I gulped. Was I really getting fired from Fancy Fred's? Really? "Can I ask why?"

"'Course, squirt!" He stood to his full height and clapped

his hands. "Nancy over there has a girl in high school who needs a job. She's half the price of your fancy college education, and I was gonna need to cut your hours anyway since things haven't been so great around these parts with that damn Audi dealership moving in across the street." He muttered a few more curse words, and I followed his gaze.

As if she knew I was getting fired, there Olivia stood, greeting a customer with a bottle of Evian and a drop-dead smile.

Damn it!

This was all her fault!

Or her boss's fault.

Whatever… it had all started with her, hadn't it?

And now it was ending with her.

I shoved my chair back. "I'll just grab my things."

I reached for my things only to discover the only object that was mine was the travel mug I'd brought from home with "this is probably gin" scrolled across it.

"Yeah," I picked it up. "So, um…got 'em…" My wallet and keys were still in my pocket as I silently left my stupid ass job. Damn it, I didn't even have a plant or box to carry out!

How humiliating.

With a grimace, I unlocked my old Dodge truck and crawled in. What the hell was I going to do now?

Rent was going to be due soon.

And as much as I would have loved to move back in with my parents, they were divorced. My mom was in Palm Springs, my dad golfing in Florida. I'd been on my own since I was eighteen.

I slammed my hands against the steering wheel when a knock sounded on my window, scaring the shit out of me.

It was Fred again.

I turned on my truck and hit the electric window button. Fred shoved his head inside my space with that dumbass smile on his face again. "Gonna need the keys, squirt."

"I'm not squirt," I said through clenched teeth.

His smile didn't even falter; he just shrugged. "You're young, kid. You'll land on your feet. Hey, maybe try the parts lot down the street. I heard they're giving kids an extra nickel on top of the eight bucks an hour they pay if they can salvage extra equipment."

"Yay." I deadpanned. "A nickel."

"Or two, if you're lucky." The man looked seconds away from roughing up my hair and slapping me on the cheek.

I dug into my pocket and grabbed the cool metallic key to the building. "Here."

"Okie dokie!" He pulled back. "Chin up, squirt!"

I had a sudden image of me yelling, "I'm not squirt," then tackling him to the ground as I punched the smile right off his face. The daydream was better than naked tits…" I shook myself out of it and sent the window sailing back up as I quickly pulled out of the parking lot, completely and utterly fucked.

CHAPTER Two

Olivia

"Lucky bastard," I whispered under my breath. Mark was getting sent home early.

In the last year, I'd seen him greet customers, wearing whatever the hell he wanted, coming in an hour later than I had to and leaving at six when I had to stay until eight, which was ridiculous by the way, because most customers came in either during the day or right after work. Rarely did we have anyone I needed to greet at eight. Rarely was anyone even in the showroom other than some of the diehard salesmen who refused to go home even if it wasn't their shift.

I squeezed the Evian bottle with my right hand, condensation dripping down the sides.

He'd lucked out.

He had gotten the easy job.

The one where he could probably eat at his desk and spike

his own coffee and nobody would so much as blink, whereas I—

I adjusted my Spanx—again. And tried to take a deep breath. I had to wear black every day, and unfortunately for me, all my black dresses were a bit too small.

I blamed being single and using my parents' Netflix and their Postmates account to deliver food, but really, I was stuck in a rut. I knew it. My friend Amelia knew it. It was just, this was not how I saw my life going.

I was driven.

And I knew that I was even overqualified at times, but the best jobs were going to people with experience or master's degrees. Nobody really cared about a business major and how good her grades had been through all four years of studying.

If anything, my lack of experience worked harder against me than if I had failed all my classes.

A little growl escaped my lips when Mark's truck disappeared down the street. He was probably getting out early so he could hang out with friends, which he still had because he got off on time. Meanwhile, I hadn't seen Amelia since last weekend, and even then, she was acting like something was wrong and kept checking her phone. She finally came up with this lame-ass excuse of not feeling well and left me alone at the bar to fend for myself.

Well, I guess I wasn't totally by myself since Mark had stopped by to punish me with his good looks, killer smile, and all-around annoying presence.

"This seat taken?" He'd grinned.

I glared. "It was."

"Hmm, looks empty, feels empty, seems like you're all by yourself, Olive."

"Don't call me Olive. It's not my name. Amelia just left because she didn't feel good and—"

His expression darkened. "Let me guess she suddenly came down with something, oh… say around two minutes ago?"

"Yes." How did he know?

His eyes pierced through mine as a slow lazy smile appeared across his face. "Interesting…"

"What is?"

"Nothing…" he said slowly as he reached over and downed the rest of my beer, setting an empty glass back in front of me. "See ya around, Olive."

I swear I was shaking by the time he sauntered off.

My heart pounded against my ribs.

And for whatever reason, I wanted to run after him, climb his body like a tree, then wrap my legs around his waist. It would be a moment of pure sexual need fulfillment followed by his death.

I'd black widow him.

But I'd at least I'd know what all the fuss was about.

Nobody was that good at sex. Nobody.

"Olivia!" My boss Mathew came jogging down the hall in his perfect black suit with his dark hair swept to the side and his tanned skin glowing like he'd just got back from the beach. Could his sparkling white teeth be any more capped?

"Yes?" I met his gaze.

He was in his late thirties, had two kids, and a wife who was a walking poster for fillers. To this day, I still had no clue if she was older or younger than him.

"Glad I caught you before you left…" He motioned me into the downstairs finance office; it was empty as he led me toward the large wooden desk.

He sat in the chair behind the desk and smiled. "You've been doing a really good job, Olivia."

"Wow, thank you." I beamed, glad he appreciated all the little extra things I'd been doing around the place. Whether it be making sure the snack section of the waiting room was constantly full or water bottles handed out to the sales floor when it was hot, but I'd been trying.

"In fact—" He stood abruptly and moved behind me to close the one massive blind that overlooked the sales floor. "—I have a proposition for you..."

Proposition almost sounded like promotion! I didn't want to get my hopes up, but I sat straighter in my chair, my lips parting ready to accept, when I felt his hand touch the back of my neck as he leaned down behind me and whispered, "You want to move up the ladder..." He tugged a wisp of my hair as goosebumps of terror rose over my body. "Nobody has to know what you did to get the next opening in marketing... besides, most everyone's gone home." He moved to face me. His gross smile widened like I'd already given in when I was too busy freaking out and looking for an exit.

I slowly stood. "I'm not into doing sexual favors for a promotion, Mathew. Especially considering you're married."

"Oh, that." He waved his hand dismissively, a bored expression on his face. "We have an open marriage. Very open."

Disgusting. "Good for you." I eased from my chair to the door and pushed it open a crack.

"You walk out of here, and you're fired," he threatened in a low voice.

"Guess I am, you asshole," I muttered under my breath as I walked to my desk and grabbed my purse, lunch, and coffee mug.

Tears streamed down my face as I got into my parents' Prius, ready to drive back to the house.

Guess I got off early like Mark.

Only I got fired.

And he still had a job.

Pissed, I made an abrupt turn off the main highway and headed toward the seedy bar Amelia and I frequented. It was a short drive, and in under two minutes, I made it to the parking lot, where I parked and cut the engine. In a full-on fury, I climbed out and slammed the door, stomping my heels as I crossed the lot and jerked open the door. Squinting until my eyes adjusted to the dim lighting, I continued stomping my way to the bar, ready to rage at the bartender and use him or her as my therapist.

"Double," I announced before the bartender could ask.

The bartender smirked. "Of?"

Could he tell I didn't do this often? "Wh-whiskey."

He sighed in annoyance. "What kind of whiskey?"

"Oh well…" I thought about it. "What kinds do you h—"

"She'll have Maker's Mark," came a familiar voice behind me.

With a groan, I turned around to see my nemesis holding a beer and smiling at me like this was the best day of his life.

"Mark," I said in a chilly voice.

"Olivia," he deadpanned and then took the seat next to me. "What brings you to this side of town so early in the day?"

I had a vibrant daydream of clocking him in the face with my purse before answering. "If you must know, I chose to quit my job after my boss came on to me…he made it sound like I would get a promotion; you know all I have to do is suck old man dick."

Mark choked on his next drink and started coughing. "Are you fucking kidding me?"

"No." My eyes did that watery thing again, which was so not crying! "I mean, I wish I was kidding, so I left, and rather than go to my parents' house at five announcing my failure as a college graduate, I ended up here, at the dive bar. I'm sure they'd be proud."

Mark shoved the shot glass into my face. "Drink and forget."

"Drink and forget." I lifted the shot and swallowed; it burned down my throat.

I was rummaging through my purse for cash to pay when Mark grabbed my wrist and gently took my purse, setting it on the floor. "I'll take care of it."

"No, you don't have—"

"Stay." His eyes locked on mine with such intensity that my mouth went completely dry. "You're not the only one who's unemployed."

"Wait, what?" I scooted closer as he held up his fingers for two more shots, and then I listened as he talked about his experience at Fancy Fred's.

"He sounds like a prick," I said an hour later, tears of laughter running down my cheeks. Yeah, I might be a bit tipsy.

"Right?" Mark lifted his shot glass back, his throat moving as he worked the alcohol down,

I could almost imagine a scenario where a bead of whiskey rolled down that perfect throat, and in an effort to save all mankind from destruction, I offer to remove said drop of whiskey…with my tongue, only to find out that my touch is the only thing needed to save Mark from the zombie apocalypse. Well, that and my body.

All of a sudden, I see hands in front of my face. Mark's huge hands. "Yo, you literally just spaced out for a solid three minutes."

"Too much of this." I jabbed a finger at the shots.

Mark smirked and then unsteadily stood, snatched my keys from the counter, and did something on his cell.

"Gotta pee," I blurted, then stumbled toward the bathroom feeling like my mind was going to explode. Was I having a panic attack? Was it the alcohol? And why the hell was I smiling at myself in the mirror? I did my business then came back to the bar top almost missing the stool as I plopped down and smiled.

"Heyyyyyy." I leaned toward him.

"Heyyyyyy." He copied me. "I'm calling us an Uber, all right?"

"Good idea." I yawned. "I need a Red Bull. 'Scuse me, sir?" I rapped my knuckles on the countertop. "A Red Bull?"

One came sliding down the bar top. Mark intercepted it, cracked it open, chugged half, then handed it to me.

I grumbled something like germs and then felt my entire body tense up when I put the can to my mouth.

It was almost like kissing him.

What was I thinking?

I hated him!

I did not want to kiss him.

Ever.

I jumped a foot when Mark's hand came out to the small of my back to steady me. "It's almost here."

"Oh, I need to pay—"

"Took care of it when you were in the bathroom," he said simply.

"But the Red Bull," I argued.

"I slid him a five. We're all good." He put his hands on my shoulders and led me out of the bar into the night.

It was still lightish out even though it was around eight.

A nice black chevy SUV pulled up. "You Mark?"

"Yup." Mark opened my door for me. I slid across the leather, suddenly exhausted, and once Mark was sitting next to me, and we were moving, I laid my head on his shoulder.

And it wasn't my imagination. He laid his head on top of mine like we'd done it a million times.

And then maybe whiskey made people hallucinate, but my hand was moving across my own lap and onto his!

Traitorous body parts!

His leg tensed, and then his hand slowly moved to my thigh, gripping it with capable fingertips, digging in just enough for me to wonder if he was going to slide his hand up.

Damn it, my Spanx!

Why did I have to be wearing Spanx?

This was the wrong time!

Bad timing.

I slowly started to pant as his hand slid higher, and then I may have let out a moan and arched a bit as he exhaled across my neck, his tongue finding a sensitive spot below my ear that had lust pounding through my system.

"My roommate's gone," he blurted once the SUV stopped in front of a nice apartment complex that I'd checked out earlier that year. It was right on a lake and newer construction.

"Okay." My mouth was making decisions my body most definitely could not cash out. I mean, right?

I was going alone into Mark's apartment.

By choice!

And he was holding my hand.

I looked down at our hands pressed together and felt like I was living outside my body; how did I get from a potential car ride home to walking into enemy territory?

He unlocked the door to 2C and let me in.

Darkness blanketed everything as the door clicked shut. I could feel his body heat as he stood behind me, then put his hand on my shoulders.

I let out a little shudder then asked, "Which one's your room?"

Mark spun me around so fast I nearly fell, only to have him brace me up against the closest wall, his mouth molded against mine.

"Can't wait," he said between kisses, and then he hiked up my dress.

Oh. Shit.

And he was holding my hand.

I looked down at our hands pressed together and felt like I was flying out of my body, lost and free from a point that made home so satisfying but entirely terrifying.

He unlocked the [illegible] and let me in.

Darkness blanketed everything as the door clicked behind [illegible] could feel his body heat as he stood behind me. Then put his hand on my shoulder.

I [illegible] a little shudder [illegible] asked. "Which [illegible] your room?"

[illegible]

[illegible] against my [illegible]

[illegible] between [illegible] and [illegible] my dress.

[illegible]

CHAPTER Three

Mark

Was I really doing this? Seducing the girl who had driven me crazy for four straight years of college only to continue on with her torture by working across the street from me?

But God, I'd wanted her since Freshman year.

She was so soft in my hands as our mouths fused together. She didn't try to force her tongue in my mouth but let me coax her into submission as I pressed my body against hers. My dick couldn't get any harder, at least so I thought.

And then, I slid my hands up her thighs and felt something. "What's this?"

"Oh shit," she mumbled. "That is, those are, I mean—"

"Are you wearing Spanx?" I asked with a giant uncontainable grin.

Her cheeks flushed bright red. "Let me just go—"

"Oh no." I kept her pinned in place. "Allow me…"

"Mark," she warned.

"Olivia," I moaned, using one hand to find the top of the high-waisted Spanx and tugging them down her perfect ass. "We all have our kink."

"Wait, what did you just say?" Her eyes widened.

"I always imagined peeling these torture devices off a sexy as hell woman and being the guy that got to kiss his way around all that punished skin, all those gorgeous, trapped curves. It's like my fucking birthday." I shuddered against her when I was able to pull the rest of the black Spanx off her feet. Then I tossed them midair and slowly unzipped the back of her dress, bringing the zipper down, down, down… until I grabbed at the front scoop neck top, pulling the loose dress off and shoving it to the floor.

She was wearing a black strapless bra, her chest rising and falling like a hummingbird's wings.

We locked eyes. Hers had always been this almost cruelly cold blue color that had me transfixed since our first fight.

My gaze finally left hers to drink in the rest of her curvy body. There were small imprints on her stomach from the Spanx. I went to my knees and pressed tiny kisses across the poor skin, while I flicked the strapless bra off with glee.

"That tickles." She squirmed beneath my mouth and then stopped squirming when I finally lowered my gaze.

I suddenly felt a bit dizzy.

How much had we drunk anyway?

She stumbled forward. I barely caught her before we fell back against the floor, her on top of my throbbing erection, completely naked.

"We doing this?" She threw her hair over her shoulder in

an attempt, I think maybe, to look sexy but just ended up making me smile at how cute she was as she tugged at the front of my jeans, freeing me.

Eyes wide.

Mouth open.

"Sorry." She wrapped a hand around my cock and squeezed. "This won't work."

"Are you talking to my penis?"

"Shhhh..." She waved me off with her free hand. "I'm having a conversation."

I burst out laughing.

We really should not be having drunken sex. Then again, sometimes that was the best kind especially when a hot as fuck girl starts talking to your cock, her mouth constantly touching the tip with her whispers. How'd she know that was a fantasy I had?

I grabbed her hand and moved it up and down.

She locked eyes with me and then very slowly lowered her mouth.

"Y-yessss." I nearly blacked out as she bobbed her head, cupping my balls and sucking so hard I couldn't think straight. "Olivia—"

Suddenly she slowed down.

And then stopped.

"Olivia?" Her mouth was still partially on me, and her head was resting against my stomach as her chest rose and fell. "Holy shit, did you just pass out with my dick in your mouth?"

Yup, taking this story to my grave.

I mean, seriously?

A snore erupted between her full lips, and then I laid back down on the carpet and let out a pained laugh.

Sadly, I got her mouth off my cock got to my feet, still feeling the effects of all the whiskey, scooped her up into my arms, and started toward the bedroom.

I stumbled a bit, swinging her body to the side. Her head collided with the doorframe before I winced and tried turning us to the side. "That's gonna bruise."

"Hmmmmm?" She opened her eyes. "That was so good."

"Yeah, the best. I rocked your world." I smiled.

"We should do that again. Mmmmm, you smell so nice, taste good too for someone I hate."

"Bad boys always taste better, Olivia, thought every girl knew that," I teased as I laid her in my bed and pulled up the covers.

"Stay!" She gripped my arm and tugged me down next to her.

So bossy.

So warm, I amended as I ducked under the covers and pulled her into my arms. So pretty.

She tucked her head under my chin and whispered, "Night, bad boy."

"Night, Olive."

"Olivia," she grumbled.

I chuckled softly. Even drunk, she corrected me.

"Olivia," I said the name reverently, then kissed her on the top of the head, passing out into oblivion and feeling content for the first time in years.

CHAPTER *Four*

Olivia

"My heeeaaad…" I mumbled as I reached for my cell, only to hit a body instead. A body?

I jolted up just in time to see Mark open his sleepy blue eyes and groan. "It's two a.m. Go back to sleep before I strangle you."

"Not before I strangle you," I grumbled under my breath.

"Would you be naked?" Mark asked and then frowned. "What are you searching for?"

"An extra fluffy pillow to hold over your mouth," I said, unable to keep the tired out of my voice.

"Olivia." He grabbed my wrist and tugged me back down against the mattress. "I plugged your phone in after I got up with a pounding headache at midnight. I also left two aspirin by your nightstand. Oh, and your mom called; I answered and told her that you'd had a rough day and are crashing at

Amelia's house, so not to worry… I'm a serious catch!"

My eye started to twitch. "You talked to my mom?"

He leaned up on an elbow and winked. "Oh yeah, and I also told her about the surprise pregnancy and shotgun wedding. Hope that's cool."

I clenched my teeth. "We didn't even get that far last night."

He grinned, all nonchalant. "How do you know?"

My memory was fuzzy, but I most definitely did have my mouth on his giant cock at one point, and I imagined it inside me. I'd closed my eyes in a vain attempt to visualize how good it would feel to have that massive thing inside me, stretching me wide and…

I gasped.

"Yes?" Mark smiled up at me. "Memory coming back?"

"Tell me I didn't." I covered my face with my shaking hands. "Tell me I didn't fall asleep on you!" Not to mention his dick. I fell asleep on it. Oh God, had it been in my mouth? Was I a sleep sucker? I could never show my face again!

The room was quiet, and then Mark cleared his throat. "I mean, it was good until you started to snore. My dick may never perform again, went into hiding right after. I mean, if he can't even get you to stay awake, he needs to really evaluate his life choices."

I groaned and fell back against the mattress. "I'm a failure at all things."

"Not all things," he said simply. "Just…you know…living on your own, getting a good job, not falling asleep during a blow job. Chin up, it's just a few things. I bet with some therapy and really intense daily practice, you could finally move out of your parents' basement and have sex without falling asleep on people."

"I loathe the moment I met you," I seethed, refusing to look in his direction.

"Too bad." He flicked my nipple before I could pull the sheet up. "I've never been so entertained since meeting you."

"Oh good, I'm like a comedy of failures. Great. Awesome. Where the hell are my clothes?"

"Somewhere…" he mused. "Did I not mention that I'm very anti-clothing in my apartment?"

"I'm sure you are." I gritted my teeth and started ripping the sheet from the bed when he tugged it back, causing me to fall across his lap.

His eyes were dancing with humor. "You're beautiful when you're angry."

"Well…" I pouted and looked away. "You're…mean."

His eyebrows shot up. "That all you got? I almost feel bad now…"

I glared. "Stop holding me hostage before I scream."

"Just like you were last night?"

My body went from cold and irritated to searing hot in one point two seconds. "I was drunk."

"Not that drunk." He bopped my nose.

Killing him.

I was going to kill him!

I lunged, only to have him move to the side so I nearly fell off the bed. He caught my arm, twisted me toward him then pressed an impressive kiss across my mouth. "There, isn't that better?"

"That's the equivalent of patting me on the head and saying 'there, there,' you condescending prick!"

"Oh honey, a nickname? This early? I'm touched." He patted my damn head again.

"Mark!" I yelled.

He grinned. "See, knew you'd yell it again."

I was going to scream.

Probably would have, but both of our phones went off at the same time.

Weird.

I scrambled away from him and grabbed mine.

He did the same.

And then I swear, in the next minute, we went from playful banter and hate sex to full-on Hunger Games.

"You, uh…" He scratched the back of his head. "Get the text?"

For the love of designer cheese, why the hell did he have to have such nice golden likable abs?

"Yeah." I tried not to flinch. "The uh, one about Emory Enterprises and the internship opening."

"They pick you?" His nostrils flared.

"Depends." I gulped. "Did they pick you?"

"I've applied three times."

"Same."

"I report in a few days."

"Damn." I kept a straight face. "Good for you."

"Olivia…" He lowered his voice and looked ready to pounce. "Did you get in?"

"Maybe." I started trying to find my clothes by way of telepathy. *Shoes, shoes, where are youuuuuuuuu?* "I should get going."

"Let me see your phone." He lunged.

I panicked and jerked back and then sprinted into the living room, hearing his footsteps pounding behind me.

And then I was suddenly on my stomach against the floor

while he pinned me there with nothing on but black boxer briefs that looked sexier than sin slung low on his hips.

"Give it!" he yelled.

"Never!" I bucked backward.

And then he was hard all over again.

And I was naked.

And he felt so good.

And I was so angry.

Possibly confused.

And the next thing I knew, he was lifting me up with his hands and pressing his tip into my entrance while I squirmed in an effort to get him to thrust harder.

When he was finally all the way in…

We both stilled.

And then, like a man possessed, he fucked me.

Hard.

Against his carpet.

With my phone in one hand.

And holding myself up with the other while he grabbed my neck, leaning down and pressing open-mouthed kisses to my skin, one hand pinching a nipple, the other keeping me pinned where he wanted me.

It was the most insane thing I'd ever done.

He was the devil.

And damn, did I want to sin.

Heaven was overrated, right?

Just let me fall in with my enemy for one damning minute.

"Mark!" I screamed. "I'm so clo—"

"Had to." He interrupted. "Needed you."

"Yes." I agreed. "Yes!"

"Enemies after this," he grunted.

"Always," I said as he pulled out and then flipped me onto my back only to surge back in, his eyes wild.

He was angelic beauty mixed with the devil.

And I was okay with it as he thrust painfully hard as if to punish both of us for feeling this attraction—for acting on it when we knew we'd go back to our corners afterward.

It was just a bit of crazed fun.

Right?

We were enemies.

Always.

But I'd earned this, right? This pleasure. As my eyes rolled into the back of my head, his mouth lowered, and then his tongue was tangling with mine, and I tasted him everywhere.

"Fuck." His hips swiveled, and then he plunged so deep I felt him in every part of my body. As I pulsed around him like my body was trying to hold him captive, he said, "Olivia, I need to tell you—"

"No." I cupped a hand over his mouth. "The line goes back." I arched. "After this…it has to."

His eyes shuttered, and then I was screaming his name as he slipped his hand between our bodies as if to finish off what he regretted starting.

I fell back against the floor panting.

Looking up at the devil or maybe a fallen angel—who knew at this point?

And then he said the damning words that I should have expected but didn't have time to protect myself from.

"You should go," he whispered, still inside me.

"Yeah," I said stunned, pulling away. "Guess I should."

I shakily grabbed the clothes strewn around the room. He watched me as I stepped into lacy panties and struggled to get my dress zipped, and smoothed as much as possible. I pulled on my cardigan without zipping the dress so I wouldn't have to muscle into my Spanx—the last thing I needed was to put on a show as sweat ran down my back while trying to roll on the damn things. Once I was safely covered, I located my shoes and put them on. I walked to the door and left without so much as a goodbye.

Hating him more than I had ever thought possible.

For being the man I'd always compare every other man to.

For being cruel when I needed him to be the bigger person.

And for agreeing to draw that line back in the sand when all I wanted was for him to say no, and keep me in his arms just a bit longer.

I didn't realize I had tears until they dripped from my chin. Until I was doing the walk of shame down the sidewalk and attempting to grab an Uber to my car.

The only thing I had to look forward to was the fact that I was an intern now for Max Emory.

Nothing, and I do mean nothing, could be worse than the walk of shame from your enemy's apartment after sober sex, not drunk, but sober sex!

Nothing.

I had no clue that a month later, I would do anything to return to this embarrassing moment.

After all, Max Emory… isn't normal.

Had I known that I probably never would have said yes.

And neither would Mark.

my dress up and smoothed as much as possible. I pulled back my cap [illegible] without [illegible] the [illegible] I would [illegible] so much [illegible] apart [illegible] I needed to put on a show [illegible] down at [illegible] with [illegible] the [illegible]. Once I was [illegible] my [illegible] dress and [illegible] I [illegible] the [illegible] and [illegible] would so much [illegible].

[illegible] thought [illegible] for [illegible] would always [illegible] every other man [illegible] the [illegible].

And [illegible] what [illegible] when I [illegible] wanted [illegible] and keep me in [illegible] a bit longer.

[illegible] they [illegible] from [illegible] down the sidewalk and [illegible] to my car.

[illegible] that [illegible]

[illegible] if they [illegible] not [illegible]

Nothing.

I had [illegible] I would [illegible] embarrassing moment.

[illegible] Embarrassed.

Had I known [illegible] I probably never would have said yes.

And that [illegible] would [illegible]

CHAPTER *Five*

Mark

"Welcome to intern initiation!" Max Emory, CEO, spread his arms wide as he smiled at the group of twelve interns, of which I was one. He was wearing a three-piece black and white striped suit. The man had friggin' spectacles attached to his suit that he randomly held up to his face looking like he belonged in the cast of A Christmas Carol. Did he even need them, or was it to throw us off his scent?

After my one-night stand with Olivia—I'd done an embarrassingly long internet search on Max and found out that he had actually been a contestant on *Love Island*. Think *The Bachelor,* but with more crazy women than any sane man would be able to handle.

Then again, Max Emory was known for being…eccentric, so maybe he'd been into it.

Some articles said that's what had sent him over the

edge. Then again, he was still happily married and a freaking billionaire, so whatever; his life wasn't that rough, you know?

Other articles said he was eccentric, both in his personal life and in work, which as he spoke, I realized was scary accurate. He was almost too confident and too happy to be torturing all of us interns.

I drummed my fingers against my thigh, waiting for the announcement, but the guy kept pausing for three seconds in between taking giant gulps of water. The hell was wrong with him?

The hell was wrong with me?

I was so nervous I wanted to puke.

I needed this internship more than I needed another night with Olivia, and that was up there with needing air.

Fuck, she tasted good.

Max droned on, and every few minutes he spread his hands wide like he was the host of some game show when there were only twelve people in the room and one camera guy documenting, according to Max, his epic speech.

Weird.

And even weirder, or should I say harder?

Olivia was here.

Two seats down.

Wearing black jeans and a gray T-shirt, looking sexy as ever.

Did she regret it?

Did she think about me the way I thought about her?

Did she even care that she made me feel cheap, so I made her angry? I mean, I was inside her when she wanted to draw the fucking line between us again as if her job was more important than whatever connection we'd had that night.

And I needed the job as much as she did.

She was no longer the girl I'd always wanted.

But the one I had to keep at a distance in order to get the job I deserved.

And I knew she felt the same way, which almost made it worse.

Like both of us were willing to sacrifice each other in order to have stability in an ever-changing job climate.

Shit. We really did deserve each other.

"Now." Max clasped his hands together, his megawatt grin huge. "Sorry about the stack of paperwork you guys had to sign."

Tell me about it. One form read, "In case of death or psychosis." What the hell?

"But we have to cover all of our bases," Max continued. "And I'm so glad to say that out of the twelve interns, two have made it through our initiation process!"

My stomach sank as I looked around the room.

One of the guys had gone to Dartmouth.

Yeah, no chance in hell I was beating him.

"A very special congratulations to Mark and Olivia! Our new summer interns!"

I froze.

Olivia paled.

So far, all great signs, am I right?

"Applause!" Max encouraged as the rest of the candidates glared at both of us like we just ran over their new puppy.

I forced a smile and a wave, not knowing what else to do.

Olivia blushed but stood and did the same like we were both in a pageant.

Even apart, we were being awkward, so how the hell were

we supposed to work so close together for the next two months?

Survival instincts kicked in as Max ushered us forward. "Come, come!"

Was it wrong that when he said come, all I could think about was her face when I was inside her?

Dirty.

Wrong.

Didn't hate the visual though.

I cleared my throat and walked toward the front of the room with Olivia walking next to me, her scent snaking around my body, making my dick twitch and my breath catch like I was back in middle school, unable to control every sexual urge I had.

My fingers flexed into two fists as I finally made it up to Max, my new boss for the next few months.

How the hell was his dark chocolate hair so shiny and thick? I frowned as he lifted his stupid ass spectacles again and examined me, then her. "Yes, you'll do just fine."

"Thanks," Olivia said with a bright smile. "Can I be the first to say how excited I am to be picked? I'll work extremely hard, I'll even stay late, whatever you need, Mr. Emory—"

"Too bad you just got a puppy that needs training, huh Olive?" I piped up. "But sir, don't worry, I have no pets, no life really; I'll be happy to spend the night at the offices if I have to. After all, nobody needs me, and the ones who say they do, like to draw super fancy lines in the sand just in case I get confused. I am a guy, huh, after all."

"Poor lonely bastard." Max shook his head. "Do you have the sads, brother?"

"Sads," I repeated. "Yes…I'm…" I gulped. "So very sad." I hung my head.

He literally pulled me in for a hug in front of everyone, then slapped my back like I was choking on a rib. "Brothers stick together. Thank you for being vulnerable with me. I'll be sure to distract you from your current life situation with work."

"It's all I want," I said with a grin.

Olivia cleared her throat. "We sold the puppy."

Max did a double take. "Into slavery?"

"No! What?" She shared a panicked expression with me then beamed at Max. "He was having a hard time adjusting to the cat, so my parents sold him, and I'm still living at home, so—"

Max held up one hand then pinched the bridge of his nose with the other. "You sold him to a puppy factory?"

"NO!" she nearly shouted. "My cousin—who's a vet, by the way—bought him from my parents because she loves puppies. I'm a puppy advocate. You won't find anyone who loves animals more!"

"Oh." Max straightened up. "That's a relief."

"Isn't it though?" She smiled brightly.

"The rest of you…" Max motioned to the room. "You can go home. You'll be compensated for your time. Thank you for applying." Everyone shuffled out as he turned to us. "Now that we're done with the official announcement…" He rubbed his hands together. "Welcome, to Emory Enterprises. Furthermore—" His blue eyes gleamed. "—welcome to the Emory Games."

My stomach flipped then fell off a cliff. "What?"

"The Emory Games." He spread his arms wide and then snapped his fingers. "Dustin, don't make me snap again!"

"Sir—" A guy in his early twenties wearing a shirt that said

Max's bitch came running with two manila envelopes in hand. "The printer's on the fritz again."

Max's eyes narrowed. "You annoy me."

"I know, sir."

"Do your hair differently tomorrow." Max flipped his wrist at poor Dustin. "And try not to cower when you get yelled at. It's disappointing."

"Right away, sir!" This Dustin guy saluted him and then did this weird mix of a march slash walk out of the room, head held high.

"I love my cousin. I love my cousin." Max repeated under his breath. "Now, please read everything in the envelopes and report to work tonight."

"Tonight?" we said in unison.

Max shrugged. "It was in the application. Must be able to work odd hours."

Odd hours meaning late hours or early ones, right? Not midnight.

"Is this the start of our workday, then?" Olivia asked.

"Read, Olivia. Read." He winked, and then he was off, but weirdly enough, the guy with the camera stayed.

I tried to ignore him as I shakily pulled out the first sheet of paper and then nearly passed out when I started to read.

Olivia and I weren't just working together.

No, Max wanted us accessible.

As of one minute ago, and as an intern, I was now moving into Emory Towers. And my new roommate?

Olivia.

Fuck.

CHAPTER *Six*

Olivia

I was going to live with him?

With. HIM?

I tried not to stare too hard at his golden biceps as he rolled his suitcase into the suite and looked around.

I had a sudden vision of me spread across him, his mouth between my legs, my breath coming in short pants.

Damn it!

I was not supposed to be imagining anything about Mark!

And yet, there he was looking sexy as hell in his tight black T-shirt and ripped jeans; I mean, *whyyyyyyyyy*? We were interns, not joining a rockband!

I snorted and then looked around with a frown as Dustin came stomping in like he was about to announce the queen.

Did the man know how to walk quietly?

He'd changed his clothes from earlier and was now wearing

head-to-toe black, including a black belt. His black eyeglasses had no actual glass, and I was busy trying to find out why, just why, when he cleared his throat and folded his hands behind his back. "Mr. Emory has left a list of your duties for the evening once you've gotten settled in."

Mark shoved his rolling suitcase down the hall and scowled. "Almost settled; which room's mine?"

Dustin's grin had me narrowing my eyes as Mark slowly started trying each of the doors down the hall, frowning as none of them opened.

"You'll be sharing the bathroom at the end of the hall, and for now, you'll share the living room."

I gaped.

Two large white leather couches sat in a gorgeous living room with wood paneling and twenty-foot ceilings. A flat-screen TV hung against the stark wall, and a long narrow fireplace occupied the space directly below it.

The apartment was basically cold and empty, beautiful but weirdly nothing I would ever pick out for myself. Maybe it was because there weren't many decorations, and things just appeared too clean.

"Both of us?" Mark asked in a choked voice. "Are in the living room? Why don't we get bedrooms?"

"You will." Dustin grinned. "Eventually. Mr. Emory is… careful in how he approaches training his interns. If you'll just read the welcome packets I've left on the kitchen bar, please. And if you have no other needs, then I'll be going."

He stomped out of the room, clicking the door shut behind him.

I was almost afraid to go over to the counter, but after seeing Mark's horrified face, I decided that I needed to appear calm and in control, not freaking the hell out that I was going to be sleeping next to him every night and working with him every day.

I had self-control.

Hah, my body has probably already forgotten what he tastes like.

I gulped.

My brain did a little chant, *oh, I know, I know!* As if it was raising its hand then shouting out for my hormones to hear, *Hot whiskey and spice!*

I made a face.

Mark backed up like I was seconds away from announcing that I would eat my own young, hands up in surrender.

Good, I was scaring the villain away.

I grabbed the key on top of one of the packets and shoved it into my Michael Kors purse that I still had draped across my body. Then I reached for the packet.

It was pretty heavy.

Huh.

"What's it say?" Mark asked.

"You can read," I mumbled, then looked up. "Or can't you?"

He gave me the finger then grabbed the other packet.

It didn't seem that terrifying, just a welcoming note from Max himself, a thank you for being part of the company.

And then I turned the page.

Mark's curse matched my gasp as we both stared at page two.

"No. Way." I hissed. "We have to test each apartment and room for maximum comfort and hospitality and offer suggestions after each evening? Wait, couch comfort? How is this not a sexual harassment lawsuit, and I'm sure as hell not testing the couch for make-out potential!"

"It's a prank," Mark announced. "It has to be."

"Um…" I kept reading. "We have to test out a total of three penthouse apartments that are meant for rich single clientele, including bedrooms. There's a freaking checklist!"

"Well, that's convenient," Mark said. "Look, we're adults, it's fine. I mean, I can understand him being anal about this, all things considered. He wants potential buyers to feel at home while still in luxury."

"Well…" I sighed, looking around. "I don't care how much money you have, this feels like a museum. They need more warmth."

"I thought so too," he said almost absentmindedly.

And then both of our eyes locked. "That was my suggestion."

"Mine too."

"Am I going to need to cover my suggestion boxes to keep you from looking over my shoulder and cheating?"

"I haven't cheated a day in my life," he sneered. "Not gonna start now."

I tapped the packet against my thigh and cleared my throat. "Not even on a girlfriend?"

"Never," he rasped.

"Oh." I licked my lips.

His eyes fell to my mouth, then back up.

My body swayed a bit.

And then the doorbell sounded, causing me to jump. I quickly walked over and opened it, thankful that it was a delivery guy with food that smelled like heaven. He looked vaguely familiar, and then it hit me when Mark suddenly spoke.

"Damon?" Mark asked. "Is that you?"

Damon had gone to college with us. I'd had a few classes

with him, but he'd hung out with Mark's group a lot.

Basically, he knew the hatred between us as well as anyone who hung out with Mark. Damn it.

Damon peered around me, eyes huge. "Mark? What the hell man, you live here?"

"Sort of?" he answered, then sighed. "It's complicated."

Damon looked back at me and grinned. "Ah, I see, complicated."

"No, no, no." I held up my hands.

"Relax." Damon shrugged. "Nothing wrong with a bit of cohabitation in a sick penthouse with enemy number one. Enjoy your takeout. And Mark?" He did that chin jerk thing guys did when they'd hit their limit on words and maturity for the day. "We should hang soon."

"Sure." Mark mimicked the movement back.

Men.

"See ya." Damon took one last look, grin wide, then walked back down the hall. I closed the door and slump-walked my way back to the kitchen. "At least they're feeding us."

"Yeah, and now Damon's going to tell every mutual friend we have that we're living together. Fantastic."

"Sorry, it's so horrifying to you." My stomach grumbled as I reached inside the bag and started pulling out all the cartons. Ah, Chinese food. "We should at least attempt to get through the rest of the packet and get along. Pretty sure blood isn't going to come out of those white couches."

"Who has white couches?"

I snorted. "Rich people who don't sit on them?"

"Probably true." He relaxed, grabbed the cartons, and moved them over to the table in front of one couch, spreading everything out like a feast then coming back for his packet.

I had no choice but to follow.

We ate in relative silence. I chose to eat first then look at the rest of the packet.

Mark, however, chose multi-tasking.

Surprising, but whatever.

He turned to the next page then started to choke.

I slapped him on the back, smack, smack, smack. He finally stopped coughing, eyes watery as he rasped up at me, "I'd say thanks, but I think you left a bruise."

"I saved your life."

"Sure." He cleared his throat. "That's what I was thinking when my ribs were puncturing my spleen—life-saving strategy, party of one."

I rolled my eyes. "What has your panties in a twist?"

"Remember that part of the intern questionnaire where they asked your preference of pet?"

I frowned. "Yeah, so? It was probably one of those personality tests like questions that check compatibility."

"Or not." He flashed me the page.

"We both chose gecko?"

"We both chose gecko," he confirmed. "It's one of our first tasks, keep the boss's pet gecko alive overnight, which at first look doesn't seem so hard, but he wants us to take shifts."

"Does the gecko actually mean human infant?"

"No, if you read here, he wants us sleep-deprived for our first mission, whatever that is."

"Well, that's rude, and say what? Mission?"

"We have five," he announced. "And after each mission a test of sorts, we won't know ahead of time what the test is or when it is, just that once we complete the mission, it will happen."

"What the hell kind of office hunger games is this?" I

murmured to myself as I started reading over the rest of the vague packet. "I mean, is there anything for us to study? Anything at all?"

The doorbell rang again.

Mark froze and whispered. "It's like The Bachelor date boxes, but a more horrifying version."

"You watch The Bachelor?" I joked.

"My mom watches The Bachelor, and I'm a good son. I'm also a heavy pourer when it comes to wine, and she appreciates that certain skill set when it's Rose week." He winked.

He was close to his mom?

My heart did a little flutter before my brain stomped on its parade, reminding me that we would be dumb to let that affect this competition.

Very dumb indeed.

The doorbell rang again.

"Shit," Mark hissed as he slowly stood.

Damn, had his thighs always been that buff? Like a trunk of a tree, made for climbing and grabbing onto—and crap, I was doing it again, wasn't I?

I refused to watch his ass as he sauntered way too sexily toward the door and jerked it open.

Nobody was there, but a small black tank sat on the floor next to a giant black bedazzled bag that said "Little G."

"Is that his—"

"Name? I'm afraid so, but why is the bag bedazzled if he's a boy?"

"Maybe he likes sparkles?"

"Yes, let's just ask him, shall we?" Mark grabbed the tank, then his bag, and closed the door.

I got up and grinned as I peered in at the lizard, which was a pale tan covered with darker spots. He had a long body with chunky legs and a fat tail. "He's super cute. Hi, little guy."

Little G opened his mouth as if to yawn then looked away.

"Huh," Mark peered into the tank. "He seems pretty chill."

"I know, right? Why would we need to stay up all night with a freaking gecko?"

"I don't know." He set the tank down at the sink then peered in the bag. "What the hell?"

Slowly he started pulling out colored ping pong balls, some weird gecko food, a blanket that smelled like a barn animal died in it, a dog chew toy, and then several containers of living, writhing mealworms making me gag.

Finally, he pulled out a small journal. "Little G's schedule," Mark announced. "At exactly six p.m. he needs to stretch his legs to accommodate the length of them. Please attach the long leash to Little G's collar and only walk around the kitchen. When he gets tired, feed him a worm. Repeat this process every hour on the hour."

"I'm calling bullshit." I narrowed my eyes at the journal. "Geckos don't need walks!"

"This one apparently does." Mark sighed. "And technically, this is our task for the night. Well, that and giving feedback on the apartment, living room, and kitchen."

My marketing mind was already churning, but then the gecko made a weird and scary screeching-hissing noise like a miniature Jurassic Park dinosaur. I let out a little scream as the bag dropped to the floor.

I knelt to pick it up and was greeted by a lovely cockroach bigger than my finger.

Shrieking, I jumped into the air and directly against Mark's hard body.

"Oomph." He stumbled back. "It's just a bug!"

"It's a cockroach!"

"So put it back in the container; it's probably part of Little G's food!"

"He'll choke on it!" I turned, still in Mark's arms. "We'll have to cut it up into tiny pieces. Not it."

"He's not going to choke—" He eyed the stationary bug. "Well, I mean, we can't kill little G by accident. Shit, if we cut it, do we cut it in half or like in thirds?"

"I think thirds?" I whispered, my focus completely on the fact that Mark's hands were holding me against him and that I could feel the warmth of his skin through his shirt.

With a sigh, he shifted his gaze downward at our touching bodies, then very quickly set me on my feet and moved to grab the cockroach. The minute he got close, though, it made a beeline for my feet. I screamed again, stomped, and then heard a crunch beneath my shoe.

"Well," Mark said with a sigh. "Guess we won't have to cut it; we'll just scrape his insides off your outsides and be in business."

"Ewwwwwwwwwww." I held up my foot. "I killed his food!"

"Good job, you're a natural hunter." Mark winked.

I made a strangled noise. "I don't suppose you'll let me wave the white flag of partnership and get the cockroach guts off my Vans?"

"Not a chance in hell, but I will video it and post it to TikTok." He smiled.

"My hero."

"I try." He put his hand across his chest. "I'll get a knife and help you dump it in his tank. "You want first shift or second?"

"Second, I think."

"Cool, let's get him fed and then find some blankets and pillows so we can start our campout in the living room."

"Great." With a disgusted face, I grabbed the knife from Mark and managed to get some cockroach guts off my person and into Little G's tank.

He started chomping away immediately.

"Aw, he likes it."

"He's got an appetite." Mark lowered his head to watch.

I did the same.

And then complete silence fell as we watched Little G eat, only to lock eyes through the damn tank for an uncomfortable amount of time.

He stared.

I stared.

Then Little G looked between the both of us as if to say, *"Yo, it's getting weird, and I'm feeling the tension, and you're ruining my dinner."*

I jerked back and walked down the hall.

Needing space between Mark and me if I was going to survive.

I heard his footsteps softly following.

I tried a few doors, then finally found one that was open. And thank God it was a closet with pillows, sheets, and blankets.

I stood up on tiptoes to reach for them, when in a classic guy move, Mark reached above me and grabbed him, his front grazing my back and my back dying a slow death wishing that move was longer than three point seven seconds.

Not that I counted.

That would be weird.

Right?

I cleared my throat. "Thanks."

"I can be nice."

"You just choose to be mean." I snorted.

"No."

I could feel the heat from his chest.

"I just choose to protect myself from girls who like to break hearts and stomp all over them."

I gasped and turned. "I'm not like that!"

He shrugged. "Okay, sure."

"I'm not!" I called after him.

"Cody, Jayden, Sawyer, Brad, and Dylan," he yelled over his shoulder. "Just in case you needed a reminder of the guys you dated in college and ruined."

"Well, that's…rude." I sniffed then stood there awkwardly, wondering how he knew every single guy I dated by name.

And why?

CHAPTER Seven

Mark

I couldn't fucking believe that I went from working at a used car dealership, getting fired, having sex with my enemy, to gecko sitting.

If I could even call it that.

The damn gecko even knew it was time for his walks when I put the minuscule leash around his collar; he even lifted his head like he could understand me.

At first, it freaked me out.

And then I realized he was a good listener, plus I was delirious from being up all night, and Olivia's shift didn't start for another hour.

I glanced at her sleeping form on the far couch. The blue fuzzy blanket had fallen partially off her body, exposing smooth legs that days ago had been wrapped around me.

I shuddered. Why the hell did the best sex of my life have

to be with her of all people?

Maybe she saw me as a player, and maybe I was, but so was she. I just refused to get into serious relationships. Meanwhile, according to Ryker, that was all she did, and every single one ended in heartbreak. Ryker did the recon and asked Amelia when I texted him to let him know that I would be living with my greatest and hottest enemy.

Damn, was it weird that sometimes I just wanted her to slap me?

Kinky.

I could be into that.

I looked down at Little G. "You ever have girl problems, little bro?"

The Gecko's mouth opened.

"Oh yeah? I bet you have all the ladies falling for your cuteness…it's just…she's just so…" I sighed. "She's… annoyingly perfect and pretty and… hateful. She's hateful, she looks down at any person who's not at her level, and it's annoying as hell."

Little G yawned. "Me too, little buddy."

I leaned down and took off his leash, then tossed it onto the counter. "All right man, let's get you back into your—"

I stopped breathing.

"Little G?" I hissed. "Come out right now!"

How was he that fast?

It was like he just disappeared!

"Little G!" I said more forcefully this time, pulling my cell from my pocket and turning on the flashlight as I searched the kitchen and hallway.

I got on my hands and knees and looked under both couches, then realized I needed more help and the lights on if

I had any hope of finding him.

"Olivia." I tapped her shoulder. "Wake up."

"Mmmmm." She grabbed my hand and pulled. "That's nice."

Goosebumps erupted along my spine. "Olivia, be serious; I need your help."

"I'll help you, baby…" She tugged me harder, and I was seriously wondering if one more night with her and a dead gecko would be worth the risk when her eyes fluttered open, and she shoved me away. "What the hell are you doing?"

"*I* was trying to wake you up. *You* were trying to seduce my hand."

"Was not!" Her cheeks blushed bright red.

"Um, yeah and you called me baby."

"I was talking about…my, my nephew! He's five months."

"Sure, hope you don't talk to your nephew like that, Olivia." I rolled my eyes. "But we have a problem."

She stretched her arms over her head, making her breasts swell beneath her tank.

My eyes were glued to her chest. "Mark? Up here."

"Yup, sorry was, um saw, like a…fuzzy."

"Good one," she deadpanned. "Now, what's the problem?"

"I can't find Little G any—" I froze. "—Olivia, don't move!"

Her eyes widened. "I think something's in my shirt."

I gave her a dirty chuckle earning a death glare. "Okay fine, sorry, I couldn't help it. Yeah, I think Little G found his way inside your bed, the little rascal."

"He's climbing up my stomach," she said through clenched teeth. "I'm a bit freaked out. Oh wait, he stopped."

"I see that." I grinned, grabbing my phone and snapping a picture. "Seems our Little G's a boob guy, aren't you, buddy?"

So this is what being a proud father feels like, huh? Gotta say I liked the feeling.

Little G nuzzled between her very perky breasts then poked his head out of the low V of her tank top as if to say, *"What? They're nice boobs!"*

No arguments there.

I coughed and looked away. "As entertaining as this is, I'm exhausted, and it's your turn for the walks. The corner by the fridge freaks him out because he can see his own reflection, almost had a gecko heart attack."

She narrowed her eyes at me.

"And he likes it when…" I cleared my throat. "When you hum."

"I'm sorry, what?" She drew back and stared, eyebrows raised.

"Humming." I coughed. "He seems to respond to it well."

"Totally curious." She crossed her arms, making her breasts pop up in a fabulous sight of cleavage, distracting the shit out of me. "What did you hum?"

"Star Wars."

"And how did that go again?"

"I'm not humming."

"I really think you should."

"No."

"Little G's getting distressed." She pointed. "Come on, one little bar…I don't want to let him down."

"We speak of this never." I jabbed a finger in her direction and earned a megawatt smile from her as she leaned in like I was going to whisper hum.

I cleared my throat and then started humming the Star Wars theme, and sure enough, Little G bobbed his head from his position between her breasts and seemed to smile at me.

Weirdest lizard ever.

"Aw, you like that little buddy," She patted his head with one finger.

I stopped humming. "Any creature would be happy as shit sitting between two Double D's and listening to Star Wars, just saying, all men are the same, apparently even across species."

Olivia shot me an amused glare. "So you're saying you're jealous of a gecko?"

"One hundred percent."

Her eyelashes lowered like she was embarrassed, and then she very carefully pulled Little G out from her top and held him on the palm of her hand. "I'll wake you up if I need anything. The couch's comfortable, you know."

Damn, I was hard.

"Yeah," I croaked. "And it looks like it's wide enough for someone to spoon so, bonus points for that."

What the hell was coming out of my mouth right now?

"Right, and we promised to test everything." She agreed, standing and putting Little G back into his carrier, then closing the lid.

I stared at the spot she'd just vacated.

It looked inviting.

Warm.

And clearly, I was insane because I barely stopped myself from diving into the couch in an effort to feel the fleeting warmth of her body against the blanket.

"Mark?" She came up behind me.

I jumped a foot and turned. "Yeah?"

"You can go to sleep now."

"Hah, right, sleep, like that's going to happen…" I forced

myself to walk slowly over to the couch and sat, grabbed the blanket then lay down, realizing that it really was big enough for two. "C'mere."

"Why?" She crossed her arms.

"Just do it."

With a huff, she made her way over. When she was close enough, I grabbed her by the wrist and tugged her into the couch, wrapping my body around her and settling in to cuddle.

Something I rarely did with anyone.

"What's happening right now?" she whispered.

"I'm testing the couch."

She wiggled her ass a bit, leaning back into my arms. "Right, then…"

She moved again.

I groaned. "What's happening right now?"

"I'm testing the self-control of the other intern…" I could feel her smile. "You know, if you break first, I get the job."

"So you've decided you can't get it on your own, ergo, you're going to stroke my dick until I pass out, then tie me to the couch and show up by yourself, showing Max that you're more punctual?"

"Good story." She moved again.

I braced an arm around her, my teeth nipping her ear. "I'd stop if I were you before I actually decide to tug down those leggings."

A whimper escaped her lips.

She kept moving.

And I kept wondering why I needed so much self-control in the first place? I mean, we were alone, and technically we needed to test the, uh, durability of all things in the apartments, right?

"I mean, we don't want to fail a test," she whispered.

"I hate failure," I agreed.

She sighed. "Is it weird that the gecko is watching us from the living room table?"

"Super weird," I said. "It's like he's making eye contact."

"I wonder if this is like porn to him?" she asked.

"The more you stare, the more he stares. It's like he froze and— what the hell are you talking about? Do you watch lizards fuck and get your rocks off?" I laughed, and then I couldn't stop as she squirmed against me.

I held her close as tears slid down my cheeks.

"Damn it, Mark! Now I'm thinking about lizard sex!"

She elbowed me dangerously close to my dick and tried to scramble away.

I grabbed her again and pressed a kiss to her neck. "I think I like hating you."

"Feeling's mutual— And… now my erection's gone because Little G just winked. I swear he winked at us." She scrambled back. "You think there's a mic or a tiny camera or something in his cage?"

We both froze.

Little G stared at us as if saying, *"you'll never know."*

"At least turn his cage around," I suggested.

She leaned in, his mouth opened.

I sighed. "He's hungry again, demolished a few of those Zoo Med snacks that came in the bedazzled bag."

"The instructions said to feed him a worm." Olivia looked over her shoulder at me. "He has snacks?"

"He's the most spoiled gecko on the planet, so yes, numerous snacks, lots of variety, quite interesting. I left the worms for you. Don't worry, though, I Googled all the snacks just in case that was part of the test, and now, even though I'm thinking about taking off all your clothes and putting duct tape over your mouth… you know, just in case I make you scream too loud, and someone thinks I'm murdering you in here… I need to sleep and get ready for our first test or game or whatever it is tomorrow, fucking Emory games."

Slowly she sat up then turned to me. Her hair was so pretty as it kissed her breasts; her lips looked almost swollen. "Try not to have any wet dreams while I'm walking around."

"Yes, how embarrassing…almost as embarrassing as falling asleep on someone's…oh wait a second!" I snapped my fingers."

She smacked me in the chest then shoved me down against the couch again, straddling me with her gorgeous tan legs.

I gripped her hips and ground her body down on mine; even through the blanket I could feel her heat.

Her lips parted as her head fell back, exposing her neck, her body moving over mine in urgency.

I didn't plan on dry humping her on my boss's couch, just like I didn't plan on putting a leash on a gecko. Maybe the best moments are the ones that surprise you.

Maybe the best moments are spontaneous, with a girl you hate but can't get enough of and want more and more despite how annoying she was.

What was happening to me?

She bit down on her lip and let out a little sob collapsing against me while I was still hard as a rock. "You bastard."

"You're welcome."

Another smack on the chest and then. "Did the gecko see?"

"Everything."

"If he has to go to therapy, you're paying," she grumbled.

I rubbed her back in small circles, then whispered, "Worth it."

Within minutes she was snoring.

And Little G looked like he needed another walk.

With a curse, I slowly disentangled our bodies, laid her on the couch, and pulled the blanket over her, then went to grab a snack for Little G. I dropped it in his cage and whispered, "No telling Max."

And I swear on all that's holy, that damn lizard, nodded his head.

CHAPTER Eight

Olivia

"Welcome!" Max was wearing a mint green suit with a white V-neck shirt underneath as he spread his arms wide from his office. "To the Emory Games!"

"Do we applaud?" I whispered under my breath to Mark.

He shot me a wink. "You applaud for his announcement and not your orgasm? I'm disappointed, Olivia."

I felt my cheeks heat. Damn it! How was I supposed to hate a guy that not only semi-forced me to ride out an orgasm but actually let me have an extra hour of sleep before taking care of the damn gecko!

"I trust Little G did well with you both?" Max nodded toward the small cage on the table.

"He was an absolute joy, sir." Mark cleared his throat.

I snorted. The little shit really was afraid of the fridge; every time he saw his reflection, he ran, and I had to run after him at five a.m. Exhausted, I ran into a chair twice and scraped my knee on the table in an effort to stop the stupid gecko not to hide under the couch…again.

If this was like having kids, then, well, no more sex for me!

Not that I had unprotected sex on the regular, but still man, I was so tired.

I swayed on my feet a bit.

"…and then you'll be expected to answer the trivia questions in order to gain enough points for the day. Remember, at the end of the internship, you'll need at least five hundred points. You'll have daily competitions, and of course, you're not only competing against each other but yourselves."

"He's crazy," Mark said under his breath, smile still plastered on his face.

"Yup," I agreed.

"So please, each of you, take a buzzer and your position as we commence with our first Emory Games event!'

"If he says Emory Games one more time…" I muttered.

Mark rubbed my back.

I almost leaned into him.

And then I jerked away.

Enemy.

I needed this job.

Get it together, Olivia! One orgasm, and you're ready to take a nap on his shoulder? No. Be cold. Ruthless. Be you!

Feeling a bit better, I stood behind my little table, quickly sucked down some of the Emory Energy Drink that was provided, and reached for my buzzer.

"And for the first question—"

"Wait." I held up one hand. "Why are we getting filmed?"

"I like watching myself." He shrugged. "And according to Little G—"

"OKAY, THANKS!" I yelled.

Max just laughed. "All right, first question. What's my favorite color?"

The hell?

Mark buzzed. "Blue."

"Correct!" Max grinned.

"That was a guess!" I shot Mark a glare.

"And a good one at that," Max agreed.

I chugged more of the energy drink. "Okay, I'm ready."

"What reality show was I on when—"

We both buzzed at the same time and yelled. "Love Island!"

"Correct, both of you are awarded ten points!"

I stuck my tongue out at Mark and waited, my finger hovering over the red button.

"Name everyone from the show Friends…"

I buzzed and answered, "Rachel, Ross, Joey, Monica, Chandler, Phoebe, and bonus points, Ben was the son, and Marcelle was the monkey."

Max looked so touched that I thought he would start crying as he dropped his cue card and slow clapped. "Thank you for being inclusive to all animals."

"Of course!" I grinned.

Mark flipped me off under his table.

Was it wrong that I clenched my thighs and imagined him flipping me off while I rode him? Was that weird? Damn it! He was messing with my head, my edge, my game!

"Next question." Max cleared his throat. "How many shell companies does Emory Enterprises have?"

Mark buzzed immediately. "Zero, you would never do something so beneath you."

"I hope," Max said, nodding, "that one day, I have a son just like you."

Mark's dimples seemed to deepen, damn him. How had I not noticed how effing hot they were?

"Last question!" Max announced. "At this point, you're behind by ten points, Olivia. If you get this question correct, you tie for the day."

I had to get it right.

Had to.

"How many licks does it take to get to the bottom of the Tootsie—"

"Commercial has three before the owl crunches down, but it's inevitable!" I shouted.

Alarms sounded.

"TIE BREAKER"! Max seemed positively giddy. "Bring in the box!"

"The box?" I repeated as someone who seemed to be more of a PA for some reality show with his headphone and mic appeared, rolling in a giant black box with a black blanket over it and a hole on either side. "What's this?"

"Step forward." Max was having the time of his life, crazy billionaire bastard; how was this real life? I kept looking for hidden cameras because this was anything but an internship, right?

Thinking I was too sleep-deprived and probably going crazy, I focused in again while Mark stared at the box like he was studying it.

"As you can see," Max said, "there is a hole on either side of this hidden box. Each of you will reach in and feel whatever object is inside this box; the longer your hand stays inside, the more points you acquire, whoever can hold their hand in there the longest, wins."

"Seems easy." Mark shrugged.

"Oh, also…" Max snickered. "It…" He smiled. "Is alive."

"Alive?" we yelled in unison.

"Alive," he confirmed. "But don't worry. You've signed all the documents, and we have an ambulance just over there." He legit pointed to the corner where an ambulance was camped out as if one of us were going to die.

What the ever-loving hell kind of internship was this?

We had signed NDAs, which meant previous interns did too, which meant when I googled, all I got was Max Emory, genius in hiring professionals.

Sigh.

Sweat started sliding down my back as my hand hovered near the dark hole. Mark eyed me, then the box, then me again, then blurted, "Is it a fucking snake?"

"Can't say." Max shrugged. "This final part of the Games begins in three…two…one."

We both shoved our hands in.

It was cold, eerily cold.

Mark's face was pale.

And then something fuzzy touched my hand. I jerked back only to realize that if I left the stupid box, I would lose. So I stared straight ahead at Mark as a bead of sweat slid down his forehead. He looked ready to pass out.

I didn't move my hand.

I didn't even breathe.

But there was definitely something alive, rubbing up on me, and it didn't feel like a kitty cat.

Oh shit! SPIDER SPIDER SPIDER! Mark must have noticed my panic because I started to shake.

"Hey, hey." Mark shook his head. "Power through, you've got this, we've got this, okay?"

I shook my head. "No," I whimpered. "I think it's a tarantula."

"Oh hell no." He uttered a vulgar curse then bit down on his lower lip. "Do they bite?"

"Yes." Max felt the need to say. "Not poisonous but painful as hell, ah good we're twenty seconds in! Well done! This is probably a new record! DUSTIN, DUSTIN, is this a record?"

Dustin came running.

Max sighed. "Why did you cut your hair?"

"Because you said it offended you when it was in my eyes." His lower lip trembled. "But I can get extensions."

"So disappointing." Max sighed. "Find out if this is a new record and go feed Hades; he's sad."

"He's...back at home."

"So drive home." Max looked heavenward. "I swear some people— oh look, you're past a minute. Good job, guys!"

I was shaking at this point.

Mark was sweating.

Slowly I reached my hand around the fuzzy thing in an attempt to grab Mark's fingers, hoping he'd understand what I was doing.

This needed to stop.

I slowly nodded my head, locking eyes with him, then tapped against his palm, three, two one.

He frowned, and then, a thank God expression appeared.

He tapped against my hand, three, two, one, we both pulled our hands out at the exact same time.

And weirdly, Max just smiled. "Well done, another tie."

I was ready to pass out when Max pulled the black sheet off the box and opened it up. When I looked in, I wanted to scream.

Two fuzzy rats greeted us with bright red eyes. "See? They only bite sometimes, don't you Stuart one and Stuart two?"

"Is there…" Mark was on his knees on the ground. "…a reason for this?"

"Yes." Max grinned. "Actually, there is. But since you've signed so many documents, I'll have to wait a bit longer until I reveal the method to my madness. Now, back to the apartments. Mark, you and Olivia are currently tied."

I collapsed back against the ground. "What the hell is this?"

Mark crawled over to me. "Actual Hell and Max is Satan."

"But once you get hired, the pay is so good," I whined.

"So good." He swore. "But do all interns have to go through this? And why are there always cameras?"

"No idea." I turned to him. "But at least he took the gecko."

"Words I never thought I'd hear a person utter," he grumbled and stood. "Come on, let's go shower."

"But not together," I added.

"No," he said quickly, and then his arm was wrapped around me, his palm, pressed against my lower back in a possessiveness I realized I didn't just want…but suddenly needed.

CONFESSIONAL *One*

Max

"Do I feel guilty?" I laughed. "Hell no, this is business, not personal. I'm the only one in the world who can match an employee up with their perfect job in less than three months. Are the series of tests difficult? Yes. Are they terrifying? At times. But it shows us how they work as a team, how they work as individuals, the tests from the Emory Games are the world's number one not talked about source for businesses to find senior-level candidates without having to ever interview at all." I grinned. "So no, at the end of the day, they'll be getting their dream jobs, so I don't feel guilty. Science has proven over and over again, for example, that taking care of a pet as if it was an infant shows your dedication and love toward what you do. On top of that, we saw today that they chose teamwork over points and stopped the box game at the same time. Everything…" I paused for the dramatics. "…is a test. But in the end. Worth it for our two shining candidates."

"And what," Rick, my producer, asked, "about the rumors that back at the apartment there was some…bonding going on?"

"Little G exaggerates. He came home with a very big smile, and that means he had a good time with his sitters. As you know we shut off the cameras in the main rooms at night. Tonight they'll be in one of the unlocked bedrooms; time will tell if they share the bed together or separate. The point is, we aren't just in the business of providing job opportunities; we also matchmake perfect personalities, so maybe they don't take the job at the end of the day, but can you turn down your one true love?"

Rick laughed. "You're an evil genius."

"Thank you." I held up Little G. "That's why I'm rich."

"Some call you crazy."

"Rick." I sighed. "Only the crazy ones make it. I'll be back tomorrow to discuss the next game. Hopefully, our contestants continue to entertain us, and I so look forward to the first streaming episode on Emory Entertainment this week."

"Another exciting surprise, your own streaming channel. How do you do it?"

"I'm an evil genius." I grinned. "Oh, and before I forget." I cleared my throat. "Max for president."

Rick actually clapped. Idiot.

We wrapped up filming, and I made my way into my camera room entertained as hell.

Olivia was in the kitchen staring at the box I'd just delivered.

And Mark still looked petrified of what could be inside.

"Let the games…continue," I whispered as I sat in my chair and watched.

CHAPTER *Nine*

Mark

"I don't trust boxes anymore." I shoved the box toward Olivia. "You open it."

She shuddered. "You're the guy!"

"Women and men are equal; not only do they deserve equal pay, but sometimes I think women deserve to be paid more for putting up with an entire male population that thinks it's acceptable to send a pic of their dick to random strangers."

Her mouth dropped open. "You're serious, aren't you?"

I crossed my arms. "As much as you 'hate' me—" I made air quotes because, let's be honest, she was rubbing herself all up and down my body last night, so maybe the hate isn't as strong anymore. My dick twitched in agreement. "—I'm not a chauvinist."

She kept staring.

I waved a hand in front of her face. "Why aren't you blinking?"

"What?" She shook her head. "Sorry was thinking… things." She gulped, and I could have sworn checked out the front of my jeans before blushing and grabbing a knife. "Fine, I'll open it but only because of the words…that came out of your mouth, that you said."

"Are you okay?" I laughed.

"Sure. Of course!" Why was she nodding so aggressively?

"Um, should you be holding a sharp object?" I asked, a bit concerned as she jabbed it into the box, cutting open the tape.

She pointed it at me. "Did you want to open the box then?"

"All yours." I held up my hands in surrender.

She snorted and then slowly pulled open one brown flap of the package and peered inside.

"What do you see?" I whispered.

"Snakes," she said with absolutely no emotion. "Lots of snakes."

"Shit! For real?" I yelled, stumbling over my feet as I reeled backward.

She set down the knife and burst out laughing. "No, dumbass, it's some sort of furniture piece from Ikea, it looks like…" She pulled out instructions and grimaced. "It looks like we get to put together a bed frame."

I nearly pounded my chest and said *I man, I use tools*, but I figured she'd just punch me in the face, so I simply nodded and snatched the instructions away from her. "Looks easy enough."

The doorbell rang again.

I paused. Sweat beaded at the back of my neck. "Think they're classically conditioning us to flinch every time someone knocks or rings?" I wondered aloud.

She laughed. "Right, like it's a social experiment we don't even know we're in."

I shook my head. "Don't give Max ideas."

I could have sworn I heard evil laughter, but it was just my own paranoia about the insane man who wore flamingo ties and who I'd one day bring coffee to.

Olivia jerked the door open, a manila envelope that had been propped against it fell inward. With a sigh, she picked it up and reached inside, pulling out a small gold key. A single sheet of yellow paper fluttered to the ground.

I picked it up and read out loud. "Master bedroom."

"Yay, a bed!" Olivia did a fist pump then seemed to remember she wasn't the only one in the room. With a battle cry, she sprinted down the hall toward the last room on the right and tried to shove the key in. When it didn't work, she panicked, dropped the key twice then moved to the next doorway.

This time the key went in, and she twisted the knob. She shoved the door open and gasped. "It's so pretty!"

I followed after her. "Oh good, a mattress. Thought we were going to have to build one of those too."

"Hilarious." She shoved me.

I shoved her back for absolutely no reason other than I liked annoying her, and I still tasted her on my tongue.

The room was huge and had another gas fireplace that had these cool looking blue rocks inside it. The walls were all white except for the wall with the fireplace. It was covered in brick and painted black.

Two plush baby blue chairs were sitting in front of the fireplace with a table in the middle. A bottle of wine and two stemless glasses sat on top, and toward the back of the room, which I assumed connected to a bathroom, was the mattress leaning against the wall framed by two side tables that I assumed they wanted to be on either side of the bed.

"Should we get started?" I asked.

She put her hands on her hips. "I guess I can't just shut you out of the room, can I?"

"You could," I said. "But then I'd be forced to do this." I opened my mouth and made a horrific screeching noise.

Olivia tackled me to the carpet in two seconds, her hands cupping my mouth, her legs straddling me.

Huh, usually when I made that noise I didn't get rewarded so quickly. I clasped my hands behind my head and grinned up at her.

She jerked her hands away. "That was so immature."

"Yup!" I agreed. "But desperate times."

"Ah…" She wiggled a bit. "That desperate to sleep in the same room with me, Mark?"

"The way you say my name, with such passion, it really does do things to me…hard things, penetrating things—"

Her hands settled back over my mouth. Okay, I deserved that one.

"You gonna be good?" she asked, looking down her nose at me, eyebrows raised expectantly.

So good she's gonna be screaming my name— Damn it! Pull yourself together, Mark!

Slowly she withdrew her hands.

I frowned. How was I supposed to think with my actual brain when she was straddling me like this?

"I'll be good." I smiled. "Now, do you want the big strong man to go get the big box and carry it in here?"

She punched me in the shoulder. "Sorry, reflex."

"Yeah, and what? Tackling me was instinct?"

"Maybe." She chewed her plump lower lip as her eyes locked onto mine with an intensity.

The doorbell rang again.

I groaned and banged my head back against the floor. "Why…"

"I'll get it." She jumped off me and left the room.

I stayed there for a few brief seconds waiting for my body to cool down, and then I desperately tried to remind myself to focus on the end game.

A job.

A good job.

A good-paying job.

Job being singular, not plural.

What if she was using seduction as a way to gain an edge? What if I was falling for it hook, line, and sinker?

And what if it was *all* a game?

I jolted up, eyes narrowed. "She wouldn't."

And then I thought about it, like really thought about it, and realized she most definitely would.

"Damn it." I got to my feet and made myself a promise not to fall for her pretty smile, lean legs, and well, there I go again.

I finally made it to the end of the hall when Olivia gave me a shy wave and pointed to the boxes on the table. "Dinner's here."

"Good, I'm starving." I reached for the box.

That was my first mistake.

Opening it was the next.

And the third mistake, well that goes back to when I was six and accidentally had a run-in with a rattlesnake and peed my pants.

"S-snake." I pointed to the snake's head in the box along with all the white meat and hit the ground.

Hard.

CHAPTER *Ten*

Olivia

"Mark!" I kicked his legs. Okay, should I have been more sensitive?

Yes.

Did I care?

Not really.

I mean, he was just lying there like the snake bit his ass, and he had no choice but to fall over and die.

And frankly, I thought he was kidding.

Until he didn't move.

And then I was worried he might have stopped breathing.

Not sure what part of our job included eating snake meat, but the instructions said it was healthy for us to try new things—whatever that meant. So I was like, *cool* cool, we'll eat some snake meat, not die (fingers crossed), then attempt to get a good night's sleep after Mark builds the bed.

But Mark was clearly MIA lying in a heap on the floor, not building the bed or being a team player.

"Marrrrk." I drew it out then gently kicked him again.

"Son of a bitch!" he roared, coming to life like I'd given him a hit of adrenaline directly down the middle of his chest Pulp Fiction style. "I'm aliiiiiive."

I staggered back. "Are you drunk?"

"Is this hell?" He looked over at the box of snakes and scrambled away like Smeagol on Lord of the Rings; I half expected him to start muttering *my precious*. "Why is this real?"

"Life?" I guessed.

"No, the fucking snake and the meat— oh shit, is the room spinning?"

"Uh, no. Maybe…" I grabbed his arm before he passed out again. "…you should just sit for a bit?"

"But protein." He shuddered. "And the bed. I'm a guy. I have to build… oh hell!" He started gagging as his gaze landed on the box with our dinner. "If you don't move the snake box, I'm gonna hurl all over your shoes, and I actually like them, so maybe we take care of that first…" He risked a closer look, and his face went pasty pale. "Oh fuck, is that another head?"

Because I also liked my shoes, I kicked the box away immediately. "Why don't we order pizza?"

More gagging.

"Do you like need…a minute?" I patted him on the back.

"Childhood trauma." He looked away. "Yeah, pizza. Now snake, the snake has to go, far, far away, can we burn the snake? Oh shit, it's staring right at me; it senses my fear!"

"It's dead."

"Its soul lives!" He scrambled to his feet and ran his fingers through his hair. "Why is this internship the worst thing ever?"

"Well..." I dumped the snake box in the trash. "If you're asking, it's all this elaborate test. I mean otherwise, it wouldn't make sense, you know?"

"Nothing, and I do mean *nothing*, about Max makes sense." Mark went to the sink and gargled some water, then spit it out like he'd actually eaten said snake and nearly gone into anaphylactic shock from the experience. "You ordered pizza, right?"

"DoorDash." I held up my phone. "Figured pepperoni was better than snake. Hey, you gonna be able to make that bed for us?"

He glared, his skin still pale. "I'm a guy, I can totally—" Tons of stumbling and the windmilling of arms.

"Did you, um, just trip on your shoelaces?"

"No. Yes. I'm a man!" he shouted. "Where the hell are the tools?"

I studied him critically. I wanted to legit win the position, not kill my opponent. "Should you be using a hammer, though?"

"AHGHHHHHHHH!" he screamed.

"Fine, fine!" I held up my hands. "Closet, go to the closet, geez."

He stomped off.

And I watched as he grabbed a toolset from the utlility closet and went into the bedroom. Seconds later, I heard pounding. Then cursing.

Then, the most terrifying of all.

Silence.

Our pizza arrived twenty minutes later, and because I felt guilty for not helping, I finally grabbed him a slice and made my way into the bedroom, expecting to find Mark somehow built into the headboard staring off into space like, *where did it go wrong? Was it during the snake episode? The cursing? The tools? And if I could do it over, would I have used that hammer or just asked for help?*

Huh.

"H-hey there, big guy," I said, walking into the dark room.

Miraculously, the bed frame was done, the mattress was on said frame along with the sheets, and Mark had tuckered himself out trying to be all manly, so there he was, lying on the righthand side of the bed.

Smiling, I walked over to him and gently laid the slice of pizza on his side.

Without even speaking, he sniffed, like a true predator, picked up the slice, took three bites, barely swallowed, then asked, "Are we done?"

"Um, do you not remember the last two hours?"

"Good pizza." His answer. "C'mere…"

I had no choice, and honestly, he looked so cute I would have chosen the same. I crawled into bed.

He pulled me against his side. "Good teamwork."

"Yup. Totally." I smiled against his warm chest.

"I hate snakes."

"I'm aware."

"But I like you…maybe I shouldn't say that, but I like you, Olive."

I would take it to my grave as I smiled against his chest again and whispered. "I like you too."

CHAPTER *Eleven*

Mark

"I'm scared of dragons, you know…" Olivia said in a sleepy voice. "No need to feel weird about the snakes."

Instantly I was wide awake. *Snakes? Aw shit.*

All of last night came rushing back, swear I had an actual episode after seeing the snake head and skin. I mean, what the ever-loving hell?

I rubbed my eyes and checked my phone, set it down, then realized that Olivia was curled up against me.

Wait, how did this happen?

And why was I questioning her warmth and awesomeness?

I pulled her closer against me. "Does this mean you hate Pete's Dragon? Because honestly," I rasped, my breathing lazy, "I really like that bro."

"Stop saying bro." Her voice floated over me.

Swear on my life, she was angelic at three in the morning. *HAH,* my brain reminded me, *but she's the fucking devil during the day, so yeah, good trade, good trade.*

"And yeah, I loved the movie they just did; I cried…why?"

"Aw…" I patted her on the head. "You actually have a soul!"

"Aw…" She twisted my nipple in her right hand. "You have feelings."

"Damn it!" I batted her away. "Honest moment, if we had one parachute, would you take it?"

Silence.

"Good times," I muttered after an uncomfortably long three minutes where she was one hundred percent not sleeping. "Thanks, by the way, for last night."

She shrugged, still not pulling away. "What do you think Max has in store for the Emory Games tomorrow, or… I guess today?"

"Other than hell, you mean?"

"Maybe he'll go easy on us?"

I burst out laughing. "And maybe you won't kill me in my sleep to gain an advantage. Sure, yeah, okay."

She wiggled against me then leaned up, her lips caressing my ear. "Could have done it way earlier, Mark, but I have this thing called…" Her tongue slid around the outside of my ear. "This thing called self-control."

"So," I choked out. "I'm alive because of you?"

"Yup."

"Gee, how do I express my thanks to the psychopath in my arms?"

"I can't even begin to imagine."

"Mmmmmm," I tugged her against me. "I can, I fucking can."

I didn't let her protest.

I kissed her.

I kissed her hard.

It wasn't a tame kiss, one where you ask if it's okay first. Nah, this kiss was all domination. This kiss was an end-of-the-world kiss, the one you give with full knowledge you may never get to kiss again, so you just fucking go for it.

"Mine." I bit her bottom lip. "Dare you to say no."

"No." She bucked against me.

"Challenge accepted." I grinned against her already growing smile as she wrapped her arms around my neck. "Damn, you feel like you belong to me, even when you hate me."

"Meh." She shrugged. "Office politics."

"Right?" I laughed. "So crazy."

"Insane," she agreed.

"Also, I'm gonna rate the bed a ten, the room a ten, the sheets a solid nine, so it seems fair…great bedroom, but…am I also supposed to rate you?"

She threw her legs around my body and squeezed. "What do you think?"

I hesitated and then, "Eleven."

She was silent for a breath. Then her mouth was on mine again before she pulled back and whispered, "Still hate you."

I laughed. "Congratulations, you've just fallen to an eight."

"Well, you're a seven."

"Seven, seven, seven." I bucked my hips against hers. "If you don't get that reference, you're dead to me."

"I mean, really." She let me flip her onto her back and looked up at me with big blue eyes. "What was Monica talking about? Like which area did you think that, oh—"

I grinned. "Good question," My fingers slid between her thighs as I pinched her clit. "It's not rocket science, but…" I leaned down and pressed a heated kiss to her neck, then sucked her skin near her ear. "Still needs practice…though I weirdly only want to do it with my enemy."

"Good…because…" She lifted her hips. "…I would hate to see how you treat your friends."

I growled, and then both of us stopped talking as I gave her an orgasm that had both of us panting, with her hand wrapped around my cock.

CHAPTER Twelve

Olivia

I let him touch me.

And I wanted him to touch me more.

Instead, I hesitated, my hand wrapped around him. His eyes twinkled with what could only be understood to reflect mischief and mayhem as he slowly pried his body away from mine and walked to the bathroom.

The sound of the shower filled the room.

The light filtered into the master.

Was I supposed to follow him?

Was that an invite?

And why did I find it so sexy? His confidence that I'd just pant after him just because he knew how to use his hands!

And I didn't mean just for the tools.

I lay back against the bed and sighed.

I imagined a perfect world where water slid down Mark's

perfect body, and he let me lick each droplet off his perfect six-pack.

Maybe he was scared in there…all alone. Snakes had been known to come up through the drains!

In some…countries. I gulped.

I mean, a good human would check on him, right? After all the trauma?

I cleared my throat and stared at the bathroom door, willing it to open, and when another few minutes went by, I finally decided to check on him, like the good person I was.

I jerked open the door and froze.

He was standing there under the rain showerhead looking up at the ceiling, lips parted as droplets of water ran down his flawlessly sculpted chin, down his thick chest, his six-pack, and then…

Damn it.

How was it fair that he was so big? HOW?

As if sensing me, he looked over, and that idiot crooked his finger at me. And what did I do?

Cuss him out?

Point and laugh?

No.

I started stripping.

And then I was walking.

And then I was under the showerhead.

And he was devouring my mouth, and I was letting him because isn't life too short anyway? Why not taste my enemy? A man who, in another world, would be a friend?

Then again, friends? They don't taste this way.

They don't taste like sinning.

Or like I was falling, and only Mark knew how to catch me.

His tongue swirled around mine, and then he was tugging my ponytail out and pulling my hair. Before I knew it, I was jumping into his arms, and he was pumping into me like we were horny teenagers. He felt so big, so good, so right that I just went with it.

It happened way too fast.

Like something you excuse to your parents, oh sorry mom I just fell on top of him, and he just happened to be naked, oh and same here.

Gah, but so… good, so… good. “Don’t stop!” I screamed.

“Never.” He pumped into me, his strong thighs slapping against mine as our mouths collided in a frenzy of kisses, tongue, and need.

“Now,” I begged.

“Bossy,” he replied, slamming his hands against the tile like he needed to hold on to something other than me to go harder.

“Always!” I screamed as I climaxed, feeling him spill into me.

Panting, I opened my eyes.

He didn’t freak out like I expected or push me away and draw a line in the sand. He just kissed me once, twice, three times, and then I lost count as we kissed in the shower and washed each other.

Only to walk out of it and pretend like we didn’t just alter the games.

Office hate plainly back in place as we took our spots on the bed, each of us still breathing heavy.

I wanted to change the game even though I knew it wasn’t possible. I wanted to alter the rules for us even when I told myself it couldn’t happen.

One job.

One opportunity.

What was more important?

Us?

Or me?

Even more confusing, Mark's hand slowly found mine under the covers as we both fell into a restless sleep, and he laced our fingers together.

CHAPTER Thirteen

Mark

Well. I did it.

I liked it.

Dreamed about doing it more.

And woke up so hard that it was painful to even look at Olivia when she turned on her side, her dark hair kissing her skin.

It was still early.

And let's be honest, neither of us wanted to leave that bed. Leaving meant that things were going back to normal.

It meant we were getting dressed and would soon go play another insane Emory game for Max, all in a vain attempt to prove to him we could handle anything he threw at us.

Psychopath.

"So." Olivia gulped. "Another day in Max's world. What do you think he's going to throw at us next?"

"At this point," I rasped, "I don't think I'd be surprised if he came riding into our apartment on a velociraptor."

"Very descriptive. Nice."

I winked. "Thank you."

Her smile had always been so soft and pretty, and I'd always appreciated it just as much as her constant scowls.

"I'm surprised nobody's knocked on the door with our next instructions," I joked, barely getting the words out when the sound of someone knocking ruined our moment.

"I'll get it," she said softly. "You know, in case it's more snakes."

"Don't even joke about that." I shuddered. "I'm going to need therapy."

"Or just more sex," she teased and then blushed. "Sorry, I don't know where that came from."

"Oh? You don't?" I pulled the blankets off me.

"Whoa there, careful where you point that thing." She turned away like she hadn't just seen me naked a few hours before.

"Not my fault. Lying next to you…affects me. Hey, that's where men and women aren't equal!"

"Tread carefully, Mark, very carefully," she warned as she put on an old Black Tie sweatshirt.

"All I'm saying is that it's super easy for you to know I'm turned on or that I want you, and all girls have is this impressive way of staring right through you and making you feel the need to guess at their feelings and surprise-surprise, if you're wrong, castrated!"

"You're not castrated."

"I'm never wrong." I grinned, only to earn a smack in the shoulder from her before she walked by. "Hurry up, Mark, games to win, men to conquer."

I made a face after her.

"Saw that!"

I begrudgingly grabbed my sweats, pulled them up, and then reached for a vintage shirt and trailed after her as I shrugged into it.

She already had a box on the table and was opening it. "Got any old sports injuries, Mark?"

"Why am I afraid of this question?" I wondered out loud. "And yeah, two knee surgeries after a failed soccer career my first year of college."

She frowned down at the box then looked up. "I didn't know you were a collegiate athlete."

My eyebrows shot up in mock surprise. "You never asked."

"But you—" I frowned. "Were you good?"

"I was there on a full-ride, so yes?" I shrugged. "Doesn't matter anymore, though. It may have been one of the many dumb reasons I decided that in order to feel better, I needed to have sex with a lot of girls and party my way through the rest of the year, though it only lasted about two months before my dad threatened to kick my ass."

"And that was enough for you to stop being dumb?"

"Have you seen my dad?" I laughed. "The guy's huge."

"Bigger than you?"

I smirked. "So many ways to answer that question, Olivia, so many interesting ways."

"Spare me the trauma." I held up my hands. "All right, so this box has matching Spartan uniforms, both red. I get spandex, so yay me. You, at least, get normal shorts." She held them up.

"Where the hell does my dick go?" I snatched them out of

her hands and looked inside. "Half of me is going to be waving as I run past people!"

"There's a fun visual, your penis dangling from your legs as parents cover their children's eyes and scream, 'it wasn't supposed to be that sort of show!'"

I glared. "Your sensitivity toward my plight makes me warm inside."

"Always here for ya, big guy." I tossed him the full uniform and then grabbed the instructions. "All right, so big shock, today we're competing in an Emory Games favorite physical challenge called I am Sparta."

"So we die?" I choked. "Have you seen The Three Hundred?"

Olivia chewed her lower lip. "Look, it's probably going to be against all these Emory Hotel employees who sit all day and have forgotten the joy of a nice long run!"

"Do you run? Because I find zero joy when I run. I lift. Heavy things. Like…b-boulders."

"Did you stutter?"

I raked a hand through my thick hair. "I'm just a little worried after yesterday's games, and it only seems to be getting worse. Might I remind you of the snake meat?"

She scrunched up her nose. "Agreed, that was weird."

"It's all a test," I muttered. "I'm convinced of it." I walked over to her and looked inside the box. Okay, so it was more of an *I'm just gonna peer over and make sure nothing terrifying jumps out and bites my neck.*

Thankfully, it was empty.

I frowned. "That's it? That's all they gave us?"

"Oh, that and a call time." She slammed the paper against my shirt.

We had to show up at night. "Does it worry you that we're going to be competing in all things physical fitness at eight p.m.?"

"I mean…" She pulled out one of the barstools and sat. "He's eccentric…"

"We keep using that as an excuse."

"True." She yawned. "It's fine, let's just do the rest of our normal intern work and grade the master bedroom and add suggestions for…" She cleared her throat. "C-comfort."

"I think," I said as I casually traced my fingers down her shoulder to her neck. "I preferred the master bath. You?"

Goosebumps broke out across her exposed skin. She swatted my hand away. "Knock it off. We need to work."

"Yes." I sat next to her. "Because we both need this job."

"Yup." She still hadn't opened her score sheet or the notebook. Instead, she stared down at it like it was going to come alive, then whispered. "I liked the master bath too."

I let out a groan. "Killing me here."

She gripped the pen in her hand so tight it looked ready to snap in half. "You know…" She cleared her throat. "It was really dark last night, so I didn't really see all of the benefits of the bath; I mean, I'm sure there was a closet? Never saw the closet or even really used the um…towel warmer because, in a place like this, they normally have a towel warmer and vaulted ceilings and very interesting things in their…" She coughed. "Bathrooms."

Next thing I knew, she was drumming her fingertips against the countertop and glancing down the hall like there was some huge secret she had to discover, and the only way to find out was through my penis.

At least that was how I envisioned the entire thing going

down. Then again, I did semi-pass out into fantasy land when she bit down on her lip. Why the hell was that my kryptonite? Like I imagined her lips were thinking of me and how much they wanted to touch me, to suck, maybe lick—oh hell.

"Yeah, me too. Let's…go…it's for science." I jerked her out of her chair, and what do you know it, my enemy came willingly.

Hah, get it? Because…?

I was going to burn in office hate hell, wasn't I?

"We still have a few hours to work." Why was I so out of breath?

We stumbled into the bedroom and then the bathroom.

I flipped on the lights and crossed my arms, pretended to be taking in the view when really, I was taking in her reflection in the mirror. "I fucking love science."

"I got an A in Bio," she said between gasps as I reached for her hips and lifted her onto the countertops.

"Good girl." Her lower lip beckoned me as my mouth covered hers, my tongue tasting hers in a way that felt damn near primitive. "I fully believe in positive reinforcement."

She gripped my head like a vise between her hands. "Then do that again."

I didn't need to be asked twice to do what I'd been fantasizing about since running into her freshman year. I tugged her lip between my teeth then sucked her the way I wanted her to suck me all the while she wrapped her legs around my body and held me so violently tight that I winced.

It was a good wince though.

One that promised some pleasure later as her small hands gripped my shirt, twisting it between her hands like she needed me to be both closer and unclothed.

"Are we crazy?" I said between hasty kisses and heavy pants.

An adorable moan escaped between her teeth as she tilted her head, taking my kiss in deeper and deeper; a man could die this way with a giant smile on his face and an explosion of stars in his eyes.

"Yes," I finally said, my voice cracked with emotion, because as crazy as this felt, it was right, so damn right, and the only way this was even happening was because we were competing, just like our tongues were right now, just like our bodies were fighting to take control.

"Countertops." My chest heaved. "Very sturdy."

"Agreed." She kissed me again.

I lifted her off the counter and walked her backward into the walk-in closet, then pressed her up against the back wall, tugging her shirt over her head with one hand. "Lighting, also nice."

"Not too bright." She reached a hand between us, sliding my sweats past my hips as my cock bobbed against her bare stomach.

I never realized I could want someone so much that every second I wasn't inside her, joined with her, was torture.

She pulled away from me as I jerked down her shorts then gripped her ass. "Very, very good lighting."

Her eyes were half-lidded as she looked up at me. "Yeah, I can almost see your dick…"

I pinched her butt, then threw her over my shoulder and carried her into the next room, which was attached to the laundry room. "This should be fun…"

Without any warning my sweats came down to my ankles and my shirt came clean off.

"Wait, what are you—"

Her chilly ass hit the even chillier front of the washer. "Damn technology, getting all silent and impossibly unhelpful."

"Worried you need help now, are you?" she teased.

I flipped the button on the drier, slammed the start button as cheesy music filled the air. "I'm just testing the equipment, baby."

"Good." She grabbed me so tight I winced. "Me too."

"Damn, I'll work hard for a perfect ten."

"That's all I ask," she said as I set her on the dryer and started kissing her again; I slid my hand between her legs, testing her response begging the universe that it was something other than, that it?

She moaned my name, sucking my fingers in as the combination of vibrations beneath her body plus my fingers had her clawing at my back. "I give it a nine."

I nipped her lower lip again. "Don't be a bitch."

"Don't be a dick."

"Mmmmm, too easy to resort to the hate, am I right?"

"I could do dryer hate sex." She pressed a very unhopeful-like kiss to my lips, almost so soft it felt like it didn't happen, and then she guided me between her thighs, and the last thing I was thinking was, *wow, I used to really hate this girl.*

Then all I kept thinking was, *is this heaven? Can I stay? If I die, can I be buried here and job? What job?*

I pumped into her, fully aware that we were being immature, dumb, twenty-two-year-olds with no condom, no inhibitions, and nothing but sweat between our bodies and it wasn't the first time, nor would it be the last.

I'd always cared.

With her?

All I could focus on was claiming her.

And making sure she knew whose name to scream when she found her pleasure: mine, only mine.

Her nails dug into my back, heels into my ass as she climaxed.

I tried to stay strong.

And lost that battle quite quickly and pathetically as I orgasmed on the spot. All we had left was the sound of the dryer.

The feel of the sex between our bodies.

Sweat.

And a fairly accurate score of the master bedroom, bathroom, and laundry room, which led me to finally whisper against her mouth. "Yeah, I'm gonna have to say a nine point five for the dryer, you?"

"Six," she said quickly and then laughed. "But the man? Eh, he's getting better; I'll give him an eight."

You'd think she had just told me I was a sex god sent down to earth.

"Ass." I pinched her butt again.

She just smiled and shrugged, but this time? This time she didn't draw another line in the sand; this time…I could have sworn I was all she saw.

Terrifying when the one thing you don't want to lose but finally get—is finally close but so far away.

"Come on." I set her on her feet. "Let's clean up."

"Yes, wouldn't want to be late for the Emory Games," she mumbled.

"Especially when ours are so much better." I shrugged, then laughed as she shoved me into the wall and ran toward the shower.

CHAPTER Fourteen

Olivia

What the hell was wrong with me?

I went from what felt like a comfortable sex goddess and hateful enemy to this nervous school girl as I stood next to him, waiting for Max to make his appearance.

So far? All I felt was a bit of fear.

A huge banner stood out above the field we were standing in that read, "I am Sparta."

There were people in the stands, at least two hundred friends and family members of Max, and a dozen cameras that we were told were filming the proceedings for company morale for the many employees around the world who couldn't be here.

Made sense.

But still intimidating.

And to make everything worse?

Mark smelled like hot sex guy.

And if there was one thing I had trouble saying no to? It was hot sex guy. He went from this guy I wanted to strangle despite his good looks to this funny partner in crime that gave orgasms out like candy during a parade.

Wait, horrible example.

The way he held me, kissed, teased—I'd never had sex the way he had sex and was now starting to realize just how addicting being in the same space as Mark was. Which again, huge problem, because I found myself smiling, thinking about him, wanting to touch him, only to wonder when the other shoe would drop, when he'd say, *"Ha ha, leading you on. I WIN."*

And wondering if he was thinking the same thing about me.

See? I should be thinking about winning the game, whatever the hell that was going to be, and instead, I was worried about him!

I stomped my foot.

"Everything okay up there?" Mark pointed at my head. He wore a sexy red bandana tied around his head, his longer hair spilling over and falling across his forehead. And his lips… of course, they had to be swollen from punishing mine!

"Yeah, yeah, sure, just, nervous…" I rocked back on my black Nike tennis shoes and tried not to panic at the fact that we were told by the judges our outfits needed to be tight in order to not get caught in the race.

Race being the keyword.

"We shall die here," Mark said under his breath as a group of six employees came out paired into twos. They looked like they ate small children for breakfast, never missed leg day, and carb-loaded just because they could.

"No body fat," I whispered. "Is that a twelve-pack?"

"Avert your eyes!" Mark put a hand over my face. "He's too old for you!"

"He has gray hair!" I pulled his hand away. "Can't I at least be impressed that he's so big? Wait, he works here?"

The girl standing next to him was like this tall Amazonian woman with sleek black hair, a black sports bra, tiny shorts, and tennis shoes that made me think of the Jolly Green Giant!

"They all look…big." Mark gulped.

"We're competing against them," I announced. "And we have to win. Whatever hate's between us right now or desire to win against one another, we can't lose this, Mark! We can't!" Panic started taking over as my eyes took in the giants standing around us. "We'll have speed on our side, take in your height, mine—"

"The hell? I'm six-two. Did you just call me short?"

"Oh, I'm sorry, have you not taken in Andre the Giant over there standing next to She Ra? If not, I'll wait!" I threw my arms up.

"Who's She-Ra?"

I gasped. "You're dead to me!"

"I was kidding. I take hot women from comic books and TV shows very seriously, as should the rest of the world. Didn't Netflix re-up the show? I think I saw something about that—"

I cupped a hand over his mouth. "*Know* your audience. *Not* the time, Mark!"

His eyes flashed as I pulled my hand away. "Damn, you're sexy when you're competitive," He tugged at my shorts, his fingers digging against my naked skin. "We should wash these…together…while still clothed. In the shower…"

I swayed toward him then jerked back. "Stop that! It's distracting."

"So are you." He winked.

"That too! That wink needs to stop. We have to focus on something other than taking each other's clothes off, and I swear if you have some sort of STD, I'm killing you in your sleep. We haven't even been—" It occurred then how truly dumb I'd been. "Oh God! We've been having unprotected sex!"

I may have shouted it.

The cameras may have caught it.

And I suddenly wondered if there were mics because the audience semi-gasped all before their attention was drawn to the announcer; of course, Max Emory, decked out in his own red joggers, shirtless with an impressive and tanned body, standing next to a gorgeous woman who gave us a little wave like she was on our team.

At least one person was!

"Are you not entertained?" Max said again for the crowds.

I shuddered.

"Hey." Mark elbowed me. "I'm clean, all right? I haven't been with a girl since my last checkup, if you must know… and it's been…a bit long. Plus, I'm assuming you're on birth control. You're a smart girl, which also makes me an idiot for not checking, so I'm sorry. You're right, it was really, really dumb…" He hung his head like he was disappointed in himself, instantly making me feel bad.

I scowled. "Of course, I'm on birth control, and how long?"

His head snapped up. "Pardon?"

"How long since… you know…"

Max started introducing everyone. "Not really the time, Olivia…" His teeth clenched.

"Don't make me throw the birth control out and trap you into marriage, Mark. How long!"

Again semi-silence.

Weird.

"Twelve months, eleven days and…" He coughed out another number, but I didn't catch it since music picked up on the loudspeakers. "Shit."

"Today, our three teams will be competing against our new interns in everyone's favorite test of endurance, mental fortitude, strength, and most of all, teamwork!"

The crowds cheered.

"The winners," Max said into the microphone, gaining everyone's silence and rapt attention, "will each receive honor and the ability to call themselves champions!"

"That's it?" Mark said under his breath.

"Oh!" Max laughed. "And did I forget to mention? Two brand new cars courtesy of Reid Emory. His donation's a favorite every year. God, I love my brother, unless he's being a jackass, which is at least half the time, thus me forcing him to donate cars every year." He grinned. "But I digress. If our interns win, they will both be awarded a whopping hundred points. If they lose and also fail to understand the true meaning of teamwork…points will be retracted from their overall score, and they'll be headed to the losers' room for the evening."

"Losers' room?" I hissed. "What the hell is the losers' room?"

"We are literally primed to lose!" Mark added. "I don't take steroids, which already puts those idiots at an advantage."

"There will be a judge at each station, enjoy your mile trek through the land of Sparta, and remember, only the smart survive."

"We're smart," I encouraged. "We've got this."

"I hate my truck."

"I hate my car."

We looked at each other, high-fived, and walked toward the start line.

Max held up a horn and counted. "Three, two, one, go!"

I charged ahead and then realized that Mark's shoe was untied and nearly killed him on the spot as I yelled his name. "Mark, hurry!"

"Sorry!" He ran after me as we caught up to the rest of the group.

"Do you see the first challenge?" he called.

I blinked over at where the contestants stopped in front of a large target.

"Hatchet throwing!" Mark came up behind me. "Let me start; I practiced this in college."

"For what reason?" I yelled.

"Um, fun?" He threw the first, hitting a direct bull's-eye.

The judges kept yelling, "Three hits and run on."

"Also, they had cheap beer."

"There it is." I crossed my arms as he threw the third one.

Direct hit.

We were already past two teams when we came to an entire pool full of mud.

"Go through the mud!" a judge yelled. "The only way out is in!"

"Off we go!" I jumped in, and Mark followed as our clothes started to drag off of us. In an effort to get the heavy weight away from my body, I dumped my shirt, only keeping on my sports bra.

"Damn."

"Do not get distracted!" I yelled behind me.

"No, not that," Mark yelled again. "That!"

He pointed to a giant rope ladder with a pool on the other side that looked like you had to jump into once you reached the top.

"That's twenty feet!" I screeched.

"What? Can't swim?" he teased.

The other two teams were gaining on us. "Come on!" I reached for his hand as we started climbing the ladder, using our speed against the strong ones who seemed to be gassing really early.

Mark reached the top first and held down his hand. I took it and wobbled on top, looking down, ready to pass out.

"Hey, hey," Mark whispered so only I could hear. "You've got this. You've been wanting to drown me for years. Think of failing this as a missed opportunity."

"Well, now that you say—"

He gave me a little shove, and off I went from the platform into the deep water. From the splash as I pushed to the surface, Mark had followed.

I didn't have any time to follow through on my threat, but the minute we got back to the apartment I was turning on the bathtub and shoving his head under the water until his legs stopped moving.

"Come on." Mark swam across to the other side and reached back to help me as I threw my wet body over the pool and nearly collapsed to the ground. "Almost there."

"I hope so." Pulling air into my lungs was getting difficult as we raced along a dark dirt road lit with torches.

Finally, we got to the end, where it said Finish Line.

"Thank God."

I spoke too soon.

Without any warning, several men came out of the clearing, wearing the freakiest masks I'd ever seen in real life. They were clowns and monsters; it was like Halloween come to life and the most random thing I'd ever seen.

"Mental fortitude," Mark cursed. "They're blocking the finish line, which means we need a way to get around them."

"Are you sure?"

"If we go through them, they catch us, and the others go past us." He started looking around wildly and then grabbed my hand as we raced into the woods where there was a clearing and then a giant tree with a rope swing.

"Wait a minute, you want us to Tarzan into the finish line?" I screeched. "Like through the air?"

"Do you have any better idea?"

I was terrified of heights.

I didn't want to admit it.

Couldn't.

Then again, I mean, he'd passed out from snake meat!

Shaking, I followed him toward the tree ladder and was thankful to at least see several judges and a volunteer near the top with harnesses. Okay, so this wasn't going to be as bad as I thought.

And then we reached the top.

Assuming we grabbed the rope, I reached for it only to have the judge shake his head, "Sorry, princess, you're only halfway; let's get this harness on you!"

I had no time to think.

Or cry.

I just let them put the harness and all the other gadgets on me, along with a helmet.

"You go first." Mark pointed to the rungs that led the rest of the way up, "That way, I'm behind you, so you're not scared."

"I'm not scared," I said super unconvincingly.

"Okay." He shot me a sweet smile. "So climb."

I forced a smile back and nearly slipped when my wet hands hit the rungs. Tears filled my eyes as I climbed and climbed and climbed only to reach the final platform and see that there were four total all in posts surrounding the finish line, and we were barely in first place when we both made it to the top.

What I thought was a rope swing was something completely different; a zip line led all the way across the finish line to what looked like a buffet and beer garden.

And there was only one way down.

"Ready?" One of the volunteers tapped my helmet, then hooked my carabiner to the line and did the same to Mark as he grabbed me from behind. "All right, you're both strapped in."

"Wait!" I screamed. My eyes were dizzy as I took in the hard ground below us. We were at least sixty feet up, it felt like, maybe more? I'd been semi-terrified of jumping off the platform into the water and probably would have hesitated more had Mark not pushed me.

But now?

Now I had to friggin' jump!

"Olivia, we have to go!" Mark grabbed me tighter.

"I can't!" I started moving backward.

"Just listen," Mark's mouth was right at my ear. "Don't focus on anything else but me holding you, okay? Close your eyes; it's an adventure. When we reach the bottom, it automatically stops us like brake, all right?"

"No." I felt the tears start to well. "I'm so sorry, Mark, I can't, I can't do this." I don't know if it was the stress, the actual failure, or the fact that I was being held by my once enemy that I now had confusing emotions toward and was terrified of so many other things like failing after college, but I lost it.

Mark sighed and slowly pulled us back to the platform.

Whatever we once had between us was gone now, wasn't it? Because I couldn't jump. Maybe that had always been my problem. Where Mark jumped and hoped he didn't fail. I jumped only when I knew I wouldn't.

I sat back onto his lap as I heard the first team hit the finish line with a giant sound of crazy music and cheers.

And then the other.

And then the other.

Then silence.

Mark was rubbing my back in slow circles. "It's okay, Olivia."

"It's not okay!" I snapped. "I made us lose all because I couldn't jump off a stupid thing, and now who knows what's going to happen to us!"

His smile was sad. "You didn't make us lose anything. You tried really hard, and you got scared. I really don't want to have to remind you about the snake incident and dream building a bed frame, but if I must, I must."

I turned my head into his chest in a combo of a laugh-cry as he held me closer and kissed my forehead. "We all have fears. What's important is we face them, even if that means we pass out and embarrass ourselves in front of pretty girls and look like idiots."

"Aw, you said it, so I didn't have to!" I held him tighter.

Our eyes locked as he whispered. "As much as I used to hate you, do you ever think I'd let you fall?"

"You never hated me." I cupped his chin as a final tear fall onto our clasped hands. "Did you?"

"Only because I couldn't have you," he finally said. "Now, before I make you cry again for being so damn nice and honest. and hot, let's not forget hot."

I rolled my eyes. "You were doing so well."

"It's like a sickness. Honestly, I can't explain it." He shook his head. "Why don't we face your fear like you attempted to help me last night before knocking myself out and jump."

He was being so sweet.

So honest.

Why did he have to suddenly become the knight when I really needed him to still be the troll that kept me from going across the bridge into my employment promised land?

"Only if you go with me and don't push me…" I stood on wobbly legs.

"Always." He grinned. "We're ready now, sir."

"But the competitions over." He looked between us. "Are you sure?"

"Y-yes." I got the word out like a nervous kid standing in front of a million people at a spelling bee who forgot how to spell cat. "We're ready."

"All right." He double-checked our equipment. "But remember, the choice to jump off the platform has to be yours."

The way he said it hit me.

The choice has to be mine.

Not Mark's.

Not my parents'.

Not anyone's but mine.

"I need you to count down from three," I called back to Mark. "And hold me as tight as humanly possible."

"Counting might be hard with such a high number." He wrapped his arms around me and squeezed. "But holding you tight…I can do that, Olivia. All you have to do is ask."

"Stop being sweet. It's creepy!"

"Stop being cute. It's distracting."

My smile was a huge, terrifying thing as he counted down from three, and when he said one, I jumped, on my own, with Mark behind me holding on for dear life.

I thought nobody would be watching.

That they'd already be celebrating and enjoying their beer and stupid food, but instead, it was like they were waiting for us as I took in all the lights, the torches, the crowds, and the cheers that went up.

My stomach nearly dropped out of my body, but the feeling of being free was worth it as we made it to the bottom and jolted to a stop near another small platform.

The volunteers unhooked our equipment and congratulated us.

Which was a bit weird.

"You did it!" Mark pulled me in for a hug just as Max approached sans microphone smiling like we'd just won instead of lost.

"Good job, team." He slapped Mark hard enough on the back to dislodge a rib and then turned to me. "I'm very proud of you guys. You finished the race even though you had no reason to."

"Proud?" I repeated. "But Max, we lost?"

"Some of the best things in life are gained…by losing."

CONFESSIONAL
Two

Max

"So you seem excited that they lost?" Rick asked once we were in front of the cameras doing another confessional. "Tell us why."

I stared him down. "Isn't it obvious? They had the best teamwork. He didn't care about winning; he cared about her, specifically more than I would like two employees to care for each other in front of others."

"And now they have to spend time in the losers' room and use that same teamwork to make sure they survive the night."

"Please." I waved my hands at him. "It won't be that bad. We've only ever sent two employees to the hospital, and one had a pre-consisting condition."

Rick was silent for a few seconds, his smile confused. "His pre-existing condition, according to you was, breathes with his mouth, is that correct?"

"Damn it, Dustin, I can still hear you from here!" I shouted as my cousin, the employee in question, took notes.

"Sorry, Max, I mean sir, I mean cousin Max, sir…" he gulped. "Sorry."

God, I loved shitting with him. He needed tougher skin. Poor kid had been allergic to his own shadow when he first started working here, and now at least he flashed attitude every once in a while.

Don't worry, he was compensated well and had a company car; the kid wanted for nothing and would have died single if it not for me.

"Dustin," I said in a strong voice. "I like what you did with your hair today."

Dustin immediately touched his hair in awe as if I'd bestowed a halo on his golden locks. "Th-thank you, Max."

"I'm thirsty." I sniffed.

"Going." He sprinted in the direction of the beer garden.

"Ah!" I snapped my fingers. "What were we talking about? Oh yes, the losers' room. Well, we took it upon ourselves to create an exact replica in the apartment; the next key will lead them into that room, locking all others. They'll stay the night there then report the next day at noon for their third task before the finale."

Rick grinned. "How do you do it?"

"Take over the world? Well…" I adjusted my cufflinks. "…it's really quite easy, you see my secret…lots of sleep."

"Wow, really?"

"No, you idiot. Do you think geniuses have time for sleep? The secret is being born Max Emory—that's the secret. Now let's tune in to the lovebirds as they discover just how cozy things are about to get later tonight."

"You dog." Rick laughed.

I glared at the camera. "Wait and see, at the end of this little taping, not only will they have the best jobs and placement in the world—but a very new and romantic love interest, nothing causes you to fall harder than being forced to do bonding assignments together. Trust me, I know these things, and the signs were already there. Wow, a job and a life partner." I wanted to clap for myself.

But Rick did it for me. "You're too generous, Max!"

"I know, I know." I waved him off and stood then made my way back over to Olivia and Mark; both of them were standing next to the wine on tap.

"Hope I'm not interrupting. I just have a simple question." I cleared my throat.

"Of course," Olivia said in her usual peppy way.

Mark, however, looked irritated that I'd just interrupted them.

Interesting development indeed. I mentally rubbed my hands together. "So, I was just wondering, where would be your ideal location for work. Anywhere in the world."

"New York!" Olivia said just as Mark answered. "LA."

"All right, good to know your own minds. I'll just leave you two to carry on with your evening and know that you need to be fully clothed at the downtown New York offices at noon tomorrow for your third challenge. Oh, and if you could start turning in your apartment grading, that would be helpful."

"Nice bathroom." Mark smirked at me.

I narrowed my eyes. "Why does your smirk make me nervous, I wonder?"

"No idea," he said innocently while Olivia's cheeks flamed

bright red.

"Uh-huh." I looked between them. "Well, have fun in the losers' room tonight, interns, and try not to kill one another. Don't want another lawsuit on my hands."

"Wait up," Olivia moved in front of me. "Two interns tried to kill each other?"

I shoved my hands into the pockets of my joggers. "Actually, one threatened to kill the other, then the one threatened said not before I eat your face off and lunged for him. We had no idea she was a cannibal; then again, that's not typically a question we put on our job applications." I shuddered. "Terrifying day for all of us, especially Dustin."

"Wait, the girl was with Dustin?"

"In the loser rooms. It was a fun wedding, though, lots of cake and whatnot."

"Wait, back up." Mark's turn to be confused. "The girl that threatened to eat her partner married him instead?"

"Isn't life a gas?" I burst out laughing and slapped each of them on the shoulder, knowing perfectly well the terror and confusion I was putting into their feeble minds. "All right, see you two later!"

Mark stared after me in stunned silence; I heard him whisper under his breath. "Holy shit, she's going to cat me."

And then Olivia snorting out, "You wish I'd have my mouth on you."

Fighting commenced.

Welcome to the losers' room, my friends. May the best man or woman win!

CHAPTER *Fifteen*

Mark

After our weird argument about why New York would always be better than the West Coast and why was I running away from something, to me calling her out for still wanting that perfect job in the perfect skyrise with her perfect stupid salad lunches and high heels, well…things got progressively worse when she said I'd end up on the beach living out of a rundown Jeep wondering where it all went wrong.

And then I was like, why the hell are we even arguing?

The ride in the SUV back to the apartments was tense and weird despite our tender moments during the games.

And by the time we got to the penthouse floor, it was little to no shock to see another manila envelope with a key in it and a giant box on the floor labeled "blankets."

Mentioned nothing about pillows, though. Hmmm.

"May as well get this over with." I grabbed the envelope, letting the key drop into my hand as I moved down the series of doors, finally opening the last one and realizing it was a closet.

Oh, hell no.

Olivia followed up close behind, arms crossed. "Is that it?"

"There's barely enough space for the two of us, let alone all night."

"We'll have to stay close."

I snorted in defiance when really my body was like, *yes please, should I be the big spoon or the small? Ladies choice?* "You sure you're okay with being that close to me since I happen to like the warm weather and ocean?"

Her nostrils flared in a terrifying way that reminded me of every lesson my dad ever taught me, which almost always ended in, *even when she's wrong, she's right*! "Or is it just women in bikinis flaunting their boobs?"

I smirked and then shot her one of my best mocking winks even though it was one hundred percent true. "Hey, the only boobs I want to see are yours." I reached out only to have her smack my hand away. "What? They're nice." I cleared my throat, the facade er, fading. "You're nice."

"Well, you—" She looked flustered and ready to stomp a foot or just kick me in the dick. "I'll just go get some pillows to go with that stack of blankets.

She marched across the hall like a sergeant and made it to the master room door and, in a herculean effort, attempted to push the door open.

Nothing budged.

Not even a slight creak or movement.

The hell? We had our shit in there! And champagne! A fireplace. I'd built that damn bed frame!

"Do you still have the key?" I asked, telling myself to remain calm lest she punch me in all my sensitive places and then blame me for the locked door.

She gave me a sheepish look. "I kind of just left it on the counter. It was gone when I came back in to see you."

Wait, so was this my fault?

Hmmmm, how to tread.

Carefully, yes, my brain reminded me very carefully, while every other part of my body was like, wait one hot minute, no master, no sexy clothes, no fancy bathroom sex, no dryer? Bummer of all bummers.

I sighed and sent a mental, *sorry troops, not tonight.*

Okay, focus!

"Right, okay." I raked a hand through my longish hair. "So we just improvise and bring in the pillows from the couch; we'll still be comfortable. And hey, we could, just kidding, can't stay on the couch somehow they'll know we didn't spend time in the room of losers or shame as I'd like to call it. Are they actually watching us?"

"Even the throw pillows are huge," she pointed out.

"So grab just one," I said, irritated.

With a scowl, she snatched up one of the black ones and tossed it, then scrambled across the room and picked up a chair.

So the first of us had cracked.

Good to know it wasn't me!

"Look!" She pointed up to a blinking light behind one of the potted plants set next to the flat screen. I'd honestly seen the plant dozens of times and kept thinking, how great, the greenery looked against the wall and stupidly commenting on it in my God awful notebook that may as well been drawings of Mark plus Olivia equals love. I was starting to really hate this job and myself for being so weak and wanting her so much and actually looking forward to a fucking closet and cuddling and, aghhhhhh!

"You okay?" Olivia whispered.

"Yeah, why?" I kicked the ground with my invisible shoe since I had a sock on and looked like an idiot.

"You yelled." She reached out to me like I was some scared animal in need of love. Wait, would that work in my favor? Could I moan a bit, fall to the ground, tell her about my sprained ankle and soon to be broken heart because I wanted her and she was going to stay in New York, and my dream had always been the opposite side of the country, breathing the ocean air, seeing the sky, I mean how could she not want that?

And yet I felt my heart go, how could she not want me? Weakass bitch heart of mine needed to sit the hell down and take a time out. No, I changed my mind; he's out of the game.

No. More.

"I think it's a camera." She ignored my meltdown and pointed again. "They've been watching us. No chance in hell we can sleep on the couch and—"

The knock on the door had both of us jumping.

"Should have called that," I grumbled, already on my way to the door. As I opened it, I did a slow clap for whatever idiot had to scurry away while we solved our mystery and flipped everyone off behind their backs or, I guess, very much in front of their backs now.

I mean, what the hell?

How much had they seen?

Did the cameras ever turn off?

Had I signed something about no sexual contact with Olivia?

I was already sweating when I was back in the living room, door closed, envelope tossed onto the table.

Olivia stared me down, then wisely picked it up and pulled out a handwritten note, which she showed me then read aloud. "It's the loser room or no room at all, no living quarters, food, or internship. You'll be fired, quickly, seamlessly, as if you never existed, oh and using the pillows? Horrible idea, the security cameras, also a great thing to rate the penthouse on, will be turned off in three, two, one."

We both looked up, and the red lights were off on the only camera we could see.

I exhaled a sigh of relief, only to inhale a sigh of real fear when I realized it was just us again.

Alone.

In near darkness.

And soon to be alone in a small room, spooning, touching, licking— *Wait a second, no, no Mark.*

She's leaving. No matter what I do.

She's leaving.

I let that sink in, then sadly realized I had suddenly thought this was real, that she'd somehow stay, that what we shared was something other than this hatred turned to lust based on this insane competition that was spurring us on toward our end goal.

To be apart.

So why did it make my chest hurt? I rubbed the stupid spot where my heart was pumping hard like, *hey, wait, I have an opinion here.*

Nope. Only the brain.

Logic wins.

So I cleared my throat, schooled my features, and said,

"Hey, we should probably get to bed. It's late, and we have to report at noon tomorrow, remember?"

"How could I forget? He was so clear and concise about why..." She groaned. "All right, well, all my things are," It was like it just occurred to her she'd either have to sleep in spartan clothes or naked. "In...there."

"Same." I groaned. "I'm tired, though. I'm actually tired. Can I just— Are you okay with..." I held up my finger. "We have the hall bathroom. What if we wash our clothes in the sink using bar soap that we know we have in there? Might I add we're testing an emergency strategy?"

"Hmm..." She actually smiled.

Damn it, stop being so pretty! Aghhhhhhhhhhhhh,

"Um..." I regained my control. "We wrap ourselves in dry towels, let our clothes dry, don't touch each other, use the humidity of the room to somehow help us not mold and wake up, and pray we can get back into the laundry room?"

"Sounds like torture."

"Well, not to beat a dead horse, but it is the loser room, so..." I shrugged. "Got any better ideas?"

She flinched, even though I didn't blame her. "N-no, not really. But you should go first."

I snorted. "Right because you haven't seen me naked, you little prude ass—"

She kicked me in the shin then marched toward the bathroom, peeling her bra off in the process.

Note. To. Self. Does well with aggression.

I smirked despite my heart telling me to shut it down and started to do the same, turning on the shower and very quickly soaping myself down only to find her stepping in like a challenge. "Turn around."

"What?" She balked.

I shrugged. "I'll get your back; you have some mud there. Just turn."

Her eyes narrowed, and then she did, turn that was, and I washed her back, down her legs, washed her off, and then handed her the soap.

She repeated the same motions for me, and while it was torture having her nipples join in on the rubbing, I kept it together, I mean, I was hard as stone, but I wasn't going to give in.

Once we were both washed, I shut off the water and turned around, much to her shocked expression, as if I was a sex addict. Then I wrapped her in a towel. I waited until she was covered, then picked up one for myself, completely dried off, and grabbed new ones for her and myself, and did the same.

By the time we had our clothes washed and hanging, it was getting late, so late I was yawning each time I tried to ask if she was okay, and she was yawning back.

We made our way into the small room, aka closet, and without thinking, I lay down trying to make space for her. She lay down next to me, closing the door and only leaving a crack so we could have fresh air.

Our breathing was our music.

Our bodies our heat.

And just when I thought I was going to go to sleep, she turned and pulled me into her arms, officially making me the mother fucking small spoon.

And I would take it to my grave, lie to the government, grandkids, whoever—but I smiled and fell right the hell to sleep. Feeling. Safe.

"What?" she [illegible].

"I [illegible]. If [illegible] you [illegible] them [illegible]. [illegible]"

[illegible], and then he [illegible] that I [illegible] her back, down her legs [illegible] and then [illegible] her [illegible].

She [illegible] while it was [illegible] her nipples [illegible]. I mean, I was [illegible] but I wasn't going to [illegible].

Once we were both washed, I [illegible] me [illegible] much by her [illegible] I was [illegible]. Then I wrapped her in [illegible] covered. Then [illegible] up one [illegible] and grabbed a new one for her [illegible].

By the time we [illegible] she was [illegible] each [illegible] was [illegible] she was [illegible].

We [illegible] down [illegible] me [illegible] she [illegible] we could [illegible].

[illegible]

[illegible] our [illegible].

And [illegible] when I thought I was going [illegible] turned and pulled me into her arms [illegible] another [illegible] small [illegible].

Until [illegible] grandkids [illegible] tell them the [illegible] I [illegible].

CHAPTER Sixteen

Olivia

I fell asleep holding him against me. At first, it was supposed to be a joke, and then the next thing I knew—I was dying of heatstroke.

And it was morning.

"Why," Mark groaned as he moved away from me, "are we wet?"

It was one of those moments where you're so grossed out you don't even want to move but also moving might prove who the culprit of wherever all the wetness came from, making you want to disappear into a puddle of shame.

"I'm…" I started. "I'm actually not sure. I mean…it happens to lots of people, but, like, did you ever have an issue peeing the bed?"

"Yes. And as an adult, I've still been unable to control my urges when I'm lying next to a hot girl!" he roared.

"I am hot, like physically scorched." I sniffed. "And seriously?"

"No, not seriously." He used his foot to open the door.

I assumed, probably just like he did that fresh air would be like a mountains breeze kiss upon our faces.

Instead, it was just as warm in the apartment.

"Heating and cooling, zero stars," Mark muttered as he crawled out of the little hole we were sleeping in.

"Do not recommend," I grumbled. "So the good news, you didn't pee the bed."

"Good news neither did you." He held up his hand for a high five.

I groaned and hit it, my hand slippery from sweat. "I've never felt more disgusting in my life, and I used to work at a funeral home after hours as a janitor; nobody needs to see that much embalming fluid, nobody."

Mark started to gag.

I hit him on the back. "You okay?"

"Sorry, it's one of my things."

"Things?"

"Every time I hear the word embalm, I'm brought back to my senior year of high school and the smell of the fluid as we dissected cats. One time, some of the…" he gagged again. "Skin got caught, and my mouth was open, and the fluid just flicked right onto my tongue."

I stared at his face, all scrunched in an agonized grimace. "You know I'm never kissing you again, right?"

"Damn it, it was years ago!"

"Four and a half. My bet, it's still in your system…" I leaned in and whispered. "Lingering…"

"Why must I tell you every life story that makes you want

to run in the opposite direction?"

I grinned. "It's kinda sexy."

"Really?"

"No, embalming fluid in your mouth and you telling me about it will never be sexy, but you looked ready to cry, so I thought I'd make you feel better."

"I'm not crying; my body's crying from lack of air conditioning. Come on, we need to find out what's going on." He marched down the hall and discovered the wall thermometer; it was one of those high-tech ones that probably synced with an iPhone.

It looked extremely sleek—translation: it looked complicated, and Mark didn't seem to be the type of guy who built computers, you know?

"Wow." He tapped it.

Actually tapped it like that would fix it.

Sigh.

"It says ninety degrees." He hung his head. Was it wrong that I loved the little bit of sweat that was dripping down the back of his neck?

He was hot on his best day.

On his worst?

I wanted to lick him.

Something was wrong with me.

He wiped the sweat and made a face, "How the hell did it get so hot in here?"

"Look, there has to be some sort of…furnace room or something, right? Don't all houses have a place where the AC's located along with all the other doodads?"

He barked out a laugh. "Holy shit, did you say doodads?"

"Shut it." I smacked his chest. "Come on, we're hunting

for the man stuff that you'll probably tap with your pinky finger and go, 'Eureka it's fixed,' only to burn down the entire apartment building!"

"Okay, first off." He pushed me up against the wall. Both of our sweaty bodies were slick against each other; what should have been disgusting was so erotic a little moan escaped between my parted lips. "I never say Eureka."

His blue eyes flashed with mischief of the sexual variety.

I gulped. "And?"

"And…" His hand moved from my naked hips up to my breast. "I kind of like how it looks like I fucked you into oblivion all night when really, let's be honest, I fell asleep to snoring."

I flicked his nose. "I have breathing problems."

He smashed his mouth against mine then whispered. "It's adorable."

"I'm not adorable; I'm sexy."

"That too." He sighed and then pulled back. "I think we might pass out if we don't get air, and as much as I want to take you against the wall then the floor, quite possibly the table—" He sighed. "—we need to fix this so we can at least report at noon looking like actual humans."

"Ugh, you're right." I snuck out from under his braced arm and started checking the locked doors.

He did the same, and when I thought all hope was lost, opened one up and burst out with the word. "Eureka!"

I started laughing so hard I couldn't stop, then he joined in, leaving me to wonder why the hell hadn't we been together this whole time? When it was this easy? When it was this fun? When the sex and conversation matched each other rather than weighing each other out?

Mark actually did tap the stupid heating and cooling unit, then took a step back and swore.

"What? What's wrong?"

"You mean other than our tropical paradise?" He smirked. "Um, that."

He pointed at a black leather bag and inside? Enough money to retire on that tropical island rather than get a job at Emory Enterprises.

Mark peered into the bag.

It was thousands, if not hundreds of thousands of dollars.

I covered my mouth with my hands.

We could get new cars.

A house.

We could probably freakin' retire.

"What do we do?" I asked.

"Um, why are you whispering?" He nudged me with his shoulder. "Look, we have only one choice."

"Tell no one, spend it and buy a Maserati?" I asked in a hopeful voice.

He patted my head. "Like I said, adorable. And now, we have to take it in at noon when we report for our next assignment, all right? It was probably put here on purpose."

I crossed my arms. "Well, that's mean."

"Um, hello. Max?"

"Right," I murmured, taking another look at the bag. "But can I at least touch it?"

"Babe, I was ignoring half of what you just said because I was already taking selfies, surprised you didn't notice; also, there are a few gold bars."

I crossed my arms. "Dumb, dumb Max putting money in here. What if the interns had no moral compass?"

Mark leaned down and took another picture. "Right?"

"He's lucky we're good people!"

"Totally." He grabbed the bag.

"Hey, what are you doing?"

"Um, what we should have done minutes ago? I'm gonna make it rain, then I'm going to take naked pictures of you with gold bars strategically placed around your body. I'm not an amateur."

I threw my head back and laughed. "I like where your head is at."

"I like where your boobs are at." He shook his head. "Sorry, you're nearly naked. You distract me more than gold bars; feel proud of that."

"I actually do."

"Maybe you can add it to your resume?"

"Huh, boobs look good naked. Yeah, has a certain ring to it."

"I'd hire you."

"As your sexretary?"

Mark dropped the heavy bag; it made a heavy thudding noise as it hit the floor. Then he picked me up in his arms and swung me around. "Nah, I'd rather you be my CEO so I could come into your office every day, see you in a tight black suit, stern look. You'd probably have glasses on even though you don't need them, and you'd have your hair in a tight bun, and my only job would be to pull your hair free then swipe all the stuff off your desk while I bent you over it."

I let out a lame whimper. "That's a fantasy I have."

"Aw, babe, I'm all about fulfilling your fantasies." He kissed me hard against the mouth.

I shoved him against the nearest wall, "Damn, how could

I have ever hated you?"

"Meh, sometimes we hate what we want to love."

"What?"

"I just said that—"

I kissed him before he could answer, and weirdly enough, the bag of cash was forgotten as I tackled him to the ground and realized that some things are more valuable than jobs than money; some things just click.

And that was us.

CHAPTER Seventeen

Mark

More keys came, allowing us to actually access our clothes which was extremely distracting since we'd basically had sex on every surface in that damn bathroom.

By the time we were in the elevator up to Max's main offices, I was exhausted.

But not from the heat.

From her.

She was wicked in the ways she came up with to use those damn gold bars. It was almost indecent.

And damn, did I worship her for it.

And realized I'd be sad when this chaos was over when we weren't living in craziness together, rating a sick apartment, and taking part in Emory Games that, let's be honest, HR should have hacked out years ago!

It was really the only confusing thing about our entire

situation. Granted, rating the apartment seemed like a normal task for marketing or even sales, but adding the whole games aspect just seemed strange, and yet it was easy to see how much the employees enjoyed our torture, which begged the question, how the hell did Max get away with it?

Was it one of those cases of, *I'm a billionaire, ergo I get a billion free passes*?

Frowning, I walked out of the elevator, bag of cash and gold in one hand and holding Olivia's with the other.

A year ago, I would have taken the money and run.

Today? I would prefer to shove it in Max's face, then shove my face in Olivia's, tell her how I feel, how I've always felt despite our differences.

I'd been jealous of how easy she made everything look, from grades to friends, jobs—everything had seemed handed to her.

But now I knew that it wasn't the case.

But how do you stop hating someone from afar when the only thing you want is to love her up close?

"Ready?" I asked as we stood in front of two giant black doors with the initials ME in silver making up the handles.

Olivia went up on her tiptoes and kissed my cheek. "As ready as a person can ever be when faced with someone like Max Emory."

"Well, when you put it that way." I winked.

I reached for the M; she reached for the E as we pulled the doors open wide and walked in.

Max was standing with his back to us in a black and white pinstripe suit, hands shoved into his slacks pockets as he looked out the massive glass windows over Manhattan.

He said nothing, just stared out.

Other than one camera guy, who seemed to be filming just Max as he basked in all his rich glory, nobody was there to witness our final game.

Weird that I didn't actually feel relieved about that.

He could toss us out that window, with proof from the video guy, and we'd probably still come up as missing persons.

I dropped the bag onto the floor in dramatic fashion then winced as the gold made a seriously loud thunk against the black marble floors.

Hope I didn't crack something that couldn't be fixed with Flex Seal.

"Ah," Max said, still staring straight ahead at the window. "The sound of honesty."

I shifted on my feet as I waited for him to turn around, but he didn't; he just kept staring. "Did you touch it?"

"Yes," we said in unison. I almost reached for her hand and squeezed, but would that be frowned upon in an office environment?

"How?" Max asked.

"How?" I repeated. "How what?"

He looked over his shoulder. "How was it touched?"

Oh shit. Could he see the guilt on our faces?

I shrugged like it wasn't a big deal and said, "You know, with our hands." And other parts of both our bodies. Surprise, your gold probably has penis on it, but gold is gold, am I right?

Max finally turned fully around, his eyes were weirdly knowing like nothing got by him, and he was enjoying the uncomfortable as hell situation we'd just gotten ourselves into. "I like gold too… Don't think I've ever liked it *that* much." He smirked. "But it's to be expected when you're young and in love—"

"You were watching!" Olivia yelled.

I reached for her hand and squeezed. She needed this job too, and yelling at your boss probably wasn't a good way to interview.

Max just shrugged. "We turn off the cameras at night… and well, we don't put any in the…private areas, except…" He chuckled. "With you two, we had to stop filming altogether, wonder why that is…"

Heat crept up my neck and flooded my face. "We, um, are avid believers in…um…sport."

Max barked out a laugh. "And I thought I was the only clever one in the room. Do tell about this sport under the roof of your employer's hotel as you intern for a job…are we talking bowling? Ping pong? Damn, I love a good pong game. I'd even be okay with naked charades because, man, you gotta stay honest and vulnerable, feel me? With all the shit out in the world, sometimes it just feels good to exist in our own perfect skin." He seemed to blackout for a moment, and then he shook his head. "But I digress. Please, entertain me."

He sat at his desk and leaned back.

"So…" Olivia started then elbowed me. "We just…like… physical…"

I squeezed my eyes shut and shot my thoughts at her. *Don't say it, don't say it.*

"Exertion," she finished with a proud smile.

Oh, dear God.

I smacked my hand against my face and winced.

"What?" she hissed. "Did you have something better?"

"Olympic bed sport!" I blurted. "Sans clothes so nobody can cheat!"

"No need to shout." Max waved us both off. "You both

passed the next challenge perfectly. It was about honesty, in case you were curious why we sweat you both out and put the money in…what's that area? The heating? Cooling? Is there a fridge there?"

"But really," Olivia said under her breath. "He's a billionaire?"

"Heard that." Max snapped his fingers. "So, today's going to be your lucky day."

"Mine?" we both said in unison.

"Sure." He grinned. "You see, typically we have a finale, but because of the, um, what did you call it? Olympic bed sport, we can't film anything without putting an NC 17 rating on it, and most of our employees would suffer trauma from the amount of times people see Mark's white ass."

"Hey!" I pointed my finger at him. "I do not have a white ass."

"You kind of do." Olivia cupped her hand over her mouth, whispering.

I turned and glared. "And you have a funny middle toe!"

She gasped. "You swore!"

Max sighed, then clapped his hands. "Children, let's get back to the topic at hand. Are you so dense that you wonder why I said we stopped filming?"

"Filming," I repeated. "Filming."

"That's what I said." Max shook his head slowly. "I fear for our next generation, I truly do, repeating words and tocking on the tik."

"Um sir, it's actually TikTok—"

"I KNOW WHAT TOCKING IS! It's better than SNAPPED!"

"Chat?" Olivia tried. "Snapchat?"

Max pressed his hands to his temples like *we* were annoying *him* and not the other way around. "Think of your pets. If you go to prison, you can't visit the pets. Becca will never have sex with you again unless it's a conjugal visit. Hey, I've had a few fantasies about myself in orange—"

"Sir." Dustin suddenly appeared out of thin air. Okay, not really; he came in the door, but it was creepy. He was creepy.

"NOT NOW!" Max roared. "Unless you have my steak, do you have my steak?"

"They were out," Dustin said quickly. "But they had lobs—"

"Say lobster, and you're fired! You know shellfish makes me puffy!" Max tugged at his tie. "Do you want me to be puffy for the cameras! Do you? Do you!" He thundered.

Dustin looked unsure if he preferred one or the other and then just said. "I don't think you look puffy."

Even I knew that was the wrong answer! Do better, Dustin!

Max's eyes bulged. "So I look puffy? Is that it?"

"No, no I was giving you a compliment!"

"HAH! A compliment would be, 'wow, Max that suit fits you well!' Not, 'I do not think you look puffy'! Because the person receiving the compliment wants to be told they look AWESOME! So let me rephrase this. DO I LOOK AWESOME?"

"Sir, YES, SIR!"

"That's all I ask, Dustin. Really not a big ask. Now go wash your face. You're perspiring, and it's making me sad."

"Sorry, sir." Dustin ran off, leaving me more confused than ever as Max faced us again.

He sighed, placing his hands onto his desk as he leaned

over. "I know you think I'm eccentric, but I get things done. And you two—" He pointed between us. "—need jobs, and the only way for me to accurately find out your true potential is to put you through what I like to call intern hell." His grin was pure evil. "Not only has every, er, non-censored moment been shared with every CEO looking to hire, but around my entire company as a reminder of how they were when they were young, fresh-faced, and I would say innocent but…" He shot a look at the gold bars.

I turned away guiltily.

"So now that the internship is over before it truly ever began, and I know what you both want, allow me to present you with this." He pulled out two black portfolios and handed one to each of us.

My throat went dry as I realized it read, "Welcome Packet, Emory Enterprises."

Thank God Olivia's said the same thing!

I quickly opened it and nearly passed out. A ten thousand dollar signing bonus on top of a seventy thousand dollar salary, access to a company car, and two weeks paid vacation plus all major holidays off!

Olivia let out a scream, then sprinted toward Max and pulled him into a hug. "Thank you, thank you, thank you!"

Max grinned and gently shoved her away as she barreled toward me and pulled me in for a tighter hug. I wanted to kiss her so badly, it hurt.

"So, now that we've settled that." Max grinned. "I'll have Dustin come back in and show you the rounds, Olivia, and you, Mark, have a plane to catch."

"What?" we said in unison.

"What did I miss?" I added.

"Nothing but your dreams!" Max announced. "You said you wanted to be in LA, so I placed you at one of my premiere boutique hotels in Santa Monica. Miss Olivia requested to stay here. Your internships are finished. Welcome to Emory Enterprises. Now, if you'll excuse me, I also have a plane to catch. Mark…" He held out his hand.

I couldn't take it.

I couldn't actually even stare at it.

"But—" I gulped. "We aren't finished, you said three months, and we've only done one apartment. Weren't there several penthouse apartments? I mean, we need to finish the job, sir."

He smiled. "As I said, you did well. The employees loved you both, I'm sure you had a fun summer fling, but you're moving on, bigger and better things, right Mark?"

"But this wasn't—" I started to talk and then realized I was the only person actually arguing.

Olivia was silent.

Staring straight ahead, not at me, not at the guy she hated maybe sometimes liked, but at thin air as if it had more importance than me.

"Yes, Mark?" Max asked.

I wanted to say that I couldn't say goodbye.

But again, Olivia said nothing.

I hung my head, then turned to her, pulled her in for a kiss to the forehead, and whispered, "Tell me to stay."

She was quiet and then, "You know I can't do that."

"I'm literally begging you to without using the words." I grabbed her shoulders. "What we have is good, Olivia; you know it is. I'll find another job, just ask me to—"

She pressed her mouth against mine in a kiss that felt so

much like goodbye my stomach hurt. "We'll always have the losers' room."

"And Little-G." My voice cracked.

Why the hell did this feel like a breakup?

Why were my eyes sweating?

"Let's not forget the bathroom."

"Or the dryer," I added, unable to even look at her.

"Jet leaves in a few," Max said again. "Are you coming or not?"

No! Both my heart and my head were in agreement, but I didn't realize until that moment that you can want something with every part of you, but if that something doesn't want you back—it doesn't matter what your body is telling you.

It's a no.

And always will be.

I staggered back and realized with amazing clarity that I did hate her; I hated her for not loving me. I hated her for not choosing me. I hated her for making me feel like a fucking emotional psychopath.

I hated her still.

Maybe my hate never truly went away; maybe it just stayed hidden under a masterful plan of seduction on her part or a stupid TV show that made me vulnerable.

One thing I knew.

My hate would never leave.

Sometimes, it's the only emotion we can hold onto without fear of it letting go of us.

So I held tight.

"I'm ready," I heard myself say.

And then I was looking at her for what felt like the last time. Counting the tears as they streamed down her face.

Hating every last one for proving to me she felt something—anything other than what she was showing.

One day I'd be back in this office.

One day I'd prove to her that I was successful without her love—that I was successful with my hate fueling me.

Yes. I'd be back.

And I'd own the world.

"Mark," Olivia called after me. "We're young, try to un—"

"Understand?" I spat, looking over my shoulder. "Understand this. I. Hate. You."

Funny how in college, it was her spewing hate at me.

Post-college, it was me walking away hating her.

Maybe in Hell, we'd find our love.

Crazier things have happened.

I was numb the entire walk to the SUV, to the fancy car that led me to my future, and during my flight to my dream job, I didn't think about what I could buy with the money I'd make or about who I would date, where I would live.

I thought about her face.

And cursed her until I fell asleep.

CHAPTER Eighteen

Olivia

I watched him go.

I let him walk away.

I wanted to scream at him. We're immature twenty-two-year-olds who were given an amazing opportunity.

We had sex on a dryer, for shit's sake!

Love?

At our age?

It didn't happen, and even if it did, was it worth risking everything to pursue? A steady job? Income? It was like he'd had no clue that I came from "the perfect household." Two parents who adored each other so much that they literally forgot to pay bills. My dad even at one point decided to start his own business just so he could be home more with my mom. There was a constant saying of, all we need is love while they looked into each other's eyes, only to forget that dinner wasn't even ready. I loved my parents. I did. I just didn't want to become like them, so blinded by someone else that I forgot about responsibilities or didn't take my career seriously. To them, love was all that mattered. To me? Stability.

A job was sometimes all that kept a person from breaking.

And I couldn't afford to break.

No matter how much my heart was already breaking.

He said he hated me.

And now I needed to bury my love for him. And hate him back, cling to it, let it fuel me for what was ahead.

"You ready?" Dustin held out his hand, showing me the way to the promised land, and I walked.

I didn't like it.

I hated every second.

Which made me hate Mark even more.

Damn him!

Or maybe it was myself I hated, as I never looked back and walked into my future.

CHAPTER Nineteen

Olivia

Five Years Later

I was nervous as hell as I sat in that stupid conference room, wondering what the hell the fuss was all about. I'd finally gotten promoted to VP of Marketing, which had been my dream job, except it gave me absolutely no social life for five years.

Oh, I went on blind dates. Amelia and Ryker had basically shoved me out their door one night and said, "Have fun!"

I half expected and, let's be honest, wanted it to be Mark on the other end. Instead, it was a man twice my age who keep leering at my breasts and combing his hair at the table—what hair he had.

He'd ordered lobster, and all I'd done was thought about Max's tirade about lobster, which of course made me think about Mark, and…

Who was I kidding? I always thought of him.

I hated that man.

Hated that every time I heard a woman whisper about how hot the new VP of Hospitality in California was, like a supermodel… my teeth clenched, and my chest hurt.

The damn man's face was in every marketing campaign. I would know because I was the one who had to do all of the marketing materials with my team.

I hadn't seen him in person once, thank God. The LA team took care of all the shoots, but every single time I saw his smiling face as I approved ad proofs, I wondered what our kids would have looked like. Which was dumb.

I wondered how he was doing.

I wanted to pick up my phone, only to realize I never even had his cell number! I didn't want to go through any corporate channels; that just seemed a bad idea. And when I asked Ryker for it, he outright said "he hates you, not a good idea."

So yeah, five years later and back to square one.

Well, two could play that game!

I saw pictures of him schmoozing up to women at events in LA, heard the chatter of who he was dating—the last one was a supermodel that used to do the Victoria Secret fashion show, and man did my hate grow to epic proportions, and yet I wanted to say TOLD YOU SO!

I'd been right to accept the job. He'd moved on just like I predicted; now he had a stable career that somehow managed to make him a celebrity.

And I had…

A nice apartment.

A car.

A dog that loved me no matter what.

A goldfish that ignored me.

An empty fridge.

And blind dates while Ryker and Amelia had twins, an adorable house in the suburbs, and a tree.

God, I was jealous of that stupid tree!

I'd even gone as far as to get one of those Japanese garden things you have to comb and tend to.

And then I bought a Chia Pet.

Then another.

Then I realized I was turning into the crazy cat lady only with Chia Pets, which had to be worse since one day I found myself talking to them. In my defense, I was extremely drunk, by myself, see? It's pretty much worse!

Talking ceased around the meeting.

Good, finally.

I took a long sip of my coffee as Max walked in, rubbing the shoulders of some hotshot, and out my coffee went.

All over the table.

And over Kevin's white shirt. Oh, he too hated me, but only because I got the promotion and he didn't.

He wiped at his shirt and glared.

"Uh yes, glad you're excited, Olivia!" Max said loudly. "Everyone, I'm sure this man doesn't need an introduction! One of the youngest VP's in our Santa Monica office and now the newest President of Marketing!"

No.

Nope.

The universe wasn't that mean.

Was it?

My gaze slid around the room, seeking blinking red lights. Were we on a television show again?

Was I being pranked.

Wait one hot minute.

Oh shit! I nearly spit out another sip of coffee.

That made Mark, the guy I hated, loved, then hated, and slept with on every surface in one of the company apartments we were marketing again and refurbishing.

MY. BOSS!

Nooooooooooooo!

I sat in pissed-off silence as Max waxed on and on and—wait a second. Movement near his chest caught my eye. Did he have a gecko in his pocket?

The hell?

How was Little G even alive still?

I swear that damn gecko smirked at me then hid back in his suit pocket all before Max grinned and pointed at me as people started clapping.

Yup, missed another announcement. I looked around with a watery smile. How was this my life?

"So!" Max rubbed his hands together.

I would not look at Mark. I would not look at Mark; I would not—damn me to Hell that man was fine.

He'd filled out in all the right places.

Broad shoulders.

Big, just everywhere, don't stare at his crotch, do NOT stare this crotch, wait, was he aroused?

I frowned and kept staring.

Max cleared his throat. "Er, Olivia?"

My head whipped up. "Yes, sir, sorry what was that?"

"Someone get her some more coffee." He laughed awkwardly.

Everyone joined in.

Officially the worst Monday meeting of my life.

Thanks, *Mark*!

Mark put a hand on Max's shoulder. "I'll explain."

Yes, please mansplain to me how to do my job. The dick!

"Olivia." His voice was deeper, his jaw so square I wanted to cut cheese with it. Wait, what? How were his eyes more blue? His smile more magnetic? I'd had my mouth on that and walked in the other direction? Had I been possessed?

"Yes, Mark?" I tried to sound confident, but my voice was barely a whisper, as if I was in my own sex tape, begging him to take me across the conference table. In front of everyone.

"Our team's in charge of the refurbishments of the rest of the penthouses at Emory's main boutique hotel, Emory Towers; you remember the one?"

Oh, I was going to strangle him with his tie!

And it was too pretty to wrinkle.

"Yup, remember it quite well, actually," I said smoothly. "As I recall, the bathrooms were a bit subpar, the lighting, not super… shall we say…flattering to small things."

His eyes flashed.

Point Olivia!

"Yeah, I also recall that the rooms were somewhat frigid, unresponsive if you get my meaning? And some of those beds, wow no heat at all, it was almost like, you were sleeping with a ghost, right?"

I clenched my teeth. "Exactly, and don't even get me started on the dryers…"

Mark actually choked, then coughed. "Yes well, we won't need to worry about marketing the dryers, though I'm sure you'd be exceptional at it, considering all your time with them."

My pencil snapped in half.

His grin grew. "So shall we get started?"

"Now?" I asked.

Max laughed. "Okay then, she's just a bit tired, you know, working all those late nights, having no social life, and basically sleeping at work."

Leave it to Max to sell you out right under the table.

"For your company." I pointed out. "And it's a joy."

"You threatened to light Roger on fire last week," Max deadpanned. "For refusing to fold the—okay, you know what, fresh starts! Let's let our fantastic duo come up with some marketing ideas for the penthouses, and we'll be off!"

Yes, let's.

CHAPTER *Twenty*

Mark

We rode in a Town Car together.

You know those really awkward movie scenes where both people are staring straight ahead, barely breathing, and refuse to even touch legs?

That was Olivia and me on a severely painful level.

And the worst part?

I still wanted her.

I'd tried not to.

I'd tried everything, but therapy, which Max suggested would be the only way to get over her. He had this whole twelve-step program planned out that ended up landing me in prison—twice. Suffice to say, I stopped taking his advice when he told me I'd feel better if I talked to Hades, and when I told him I didn't believe in the underworld, he whistled, and an honest to God goat came strolling out with a collar on and red eyes.

Those eyes peered into my soul.

It was the creepiest thing I'd ever seen in my entire life.

I don't even remember running out of his penthouse. His poor wife had been making us dinner once again, and I heard her utter, "Really Max, again?"

Apparently, that was normal for them.

I shuddered and brought myself back to the present.

"Everything okay?" I asked smoothly.

Olivia sighed and looked out the window. "You're doing well."

"As are you."

"How's the supermodel girlfriend?"

"How would you even know if I have a girlfriend, checking up on the guy you slept with, abandoned, and now hate? Or just morbid curiosity since I got the president job and you didn't?"

She scowled. "It's not about that."

"Isn't it, though?"

"You walked away too!" She turned to me, all rage and perfection. Her hair was a blunt cut, darker, so dark and shiny I wanted to weave my fingers into it to feel the silk, her eyes a crystal blue, her full lips painted with a pink lipstick I wanted on every part of my body.

Five years.

Five damn years.

And I still felt ready to rip her clothes off.

But it was more than that.

I wanted everything this time.

Take no prisoners.

She was mine.

I was hers.

And well, since Max promoted me and I moved back, it

seemed like the right time. Actually, everything weirdly fell into place, even selling my apartment, which was weird since it was such a high price point I was told it would take a while.

Now that I thought about it…

"Hellooooo…" Olivia waved in front of my face. "We're here."

"Sorry, I was thinking." I nodded toward her chest. "Maybe button that top one more button, so men don't stare; that's not how we do business at Emory Enterprises."

She looked ready to throat punch me, and honestly, I wanted her to take it down a few buttons, but that would be grounds for sexual harassment, so I looked away and got out of the car.

She followed, and up both of our heads went as we eyed the building that used to be our home back when we were interns.

It was eerie being back.

And as we stepped onto the elevator and hit the first level Penthouse button—the one we'd lived in, my cock literally sprang to life like it was returning home.

Damn it.

I turned away from her but could still smell her perfume as she sighed in annoyance next to me.

"So." I gulped, turning back. "I hear Amelia and Ryker have hellions for children."

She smiled a real smile. "They're exhausting, but I love them."

"Ah, so you can love something, good to know."

"Could you not?" She glared.

I just grinned, loving her every reaction down to the way she swallowed when she was angry.

I was in deep.

I walked carefully as to not impale myself on a potted plant and make the situation worse, thankful she refused to even look at me since she'd get an eyeful as we made it to the door and shoved the key in.

"The paint's new," was the first thing she said.

"Yup." I stood awkwardly. "And the, uh, lighting, they fixed what we asked."

"Totally." She rocked back on her heels as we slowly made our way around the apartment, stopping at the master bedroom. "After you."

"No after you, I insist," I motioned for her to go through.

"No, no, you first." She laughed nervously.

"Fine." I swallowed the lump of emotion and trepidation in my throat and walked in.

Behind me, she gasped. "It's the same headboard."

"I still don't remember building it. I blacked out."

"Blame the snakes." She laughed.

I joined in, and then we were both reminiscing about everything as we walked through the master into the bathroom, past a new dryer, and back into the kitchen.

"It was intense but fun," I finally said.

"You see the new interns?" she asked.

I rolled my eyes. "Child's play. Can you imagine someone being afraid of a little obstacle course?"

"Never." She laughed.

And just like that, we were back.

The tension was so thick it was hard to breathe, and like the ghost from Christmas past, the doorbell rang.

We both jumped and said in unison. "Classic conditioning."

"Is that why he brings bells to meetings?" she asked.

"Holy shit!" I slammed the counter with my hand. "I

wondered why I started sweating and almost cried that one time—"

"You almost cried."

"Long story, you don't get to hear it." I jabbed a finger at her as she opened the door and frowned.

On the floor were a bottle of wine, two glasses, and another manila envelope.

"When will it end?" I asked no one in general.

"I wonder if that's just how he runs penthouses, through fear and foreboding. Live in this gorgeous building, I'll give you the world, but remember when the devil, aka Max, calls, you're gonna shit your pants." She laughed.

I joined in and grabbed a glass from her. The wine was already uncorked, so both of us poured a glass and stared at the envelope.

"I almost don't want to open it," she whispered.

"What? Why?" I reached for it.

She grabbed my hand and stopped me. "Because." Tears filled her eyes. "It feels like it's really over if we do. I don't want, I can't—"

I'd never seen Olivia cry so hard in my entire life.

Ever.

She wasn't a crier.

But suddenly, she was in my arms.

And I was kissing her tears.

And then she was pulling my tie loose at the same time I was jerking up her skirt.

"This is crazy," I muttered between hungry kisses.

"I love you," she whispered against my neck, her mouth pressed there where it belonged, where it had always belonged. "I thought we were too young, I thought that I wouldn't have security or money that we'd regret it, you'd resent me, I thought—"

"You did the right thing, even though I hated it." I jerked her skirt completely up. "I was immature, still am, still pass out when I see snakes, even pictures of snakes make me lose an erection, serious problem. No snake art, all right?"

She threw her arms around me. "Just don't turn around then."

"Not funny. You need this erection, don't you?"

"Oops, forgot." She wiggled against me, "Can I rip your shirt and make the buttons go flying?"

"I mean, is there any other way to do it?" I said while she reached for my shirt and ripped it open.

Her gasp was all I needed to feel like a man again. "You like?"

"What, do you have a gym in your office?" She ran her fingers down my stomach. "I'm going to name them." Then she leaned down. "My precious—"

"Okay, you've been alone way too long, need you, now."

She threw her arms around me as we stumbled back against the now *black* leather couches. Shoes went flying, inhibitions were lost, the wine hadn't even been finished yet.

Our kisses were mature.

Different.

But at the same time, more aggressive, needy, because it had only ever been her for me. "I love you too. I always have. I always will."

I didn't prep her.

I didn't need to.

She was ready for me, and I'd been waiting to be with her for years.

We joined.

And that was it.

She was mine.

I rolled my hips.

She moaned my name and hooked an ankle around me, pulling me closer as we tumbled off the couch, her on top as she rode me. Her breasts jiggled beneath her blouse, so I tore it open since they were crying *touch me.*

The vision of her riding me, of her mouth parted, her body arched to take me in, was more than my tiny brain could handle, and when she raked her nails down my chest, I exploded.

Thankful that she was right with me, always right with me, wasn't she?

Both of us out of breath, she fell against me, her hair tickling my chin. "Are we going to get fired?"

"Nah, I'm your boss. Fuck me anytime you want. Really, I'm available morning, noon, night, holidays, especially my birthday—"

She kissed me again.

And then, of course, another knock sounded.

We both groaned and quickly put our clothes back together.

When she opened the door, it was another bottle, this time it was champagne.

"What's going on?" She pulled off a sticky note that read," Open the envelope, idiots."

"Max," we both said and then sighed.

I grabbed the envelope, took a deep breath, and dumped out the contents. Inside were two keys and a note.

"What's it say?"

I started reading in disbelief and then laughed.

"What? What is it!" she yelled, smacking me in the arm.

Some things never changed; they should, but they didn't. I rubbed the sore spot.

"Dear Interns." I laughed again. "I knew you could do it. You see, sometimes it takes a few years for love to mature, like the fine wine I sent earlier, and other times all it takes is the place you fell for each other and suffered together to make you realize how much you've been suffering on your own. Please accept this penthouse as another bonus for doing such an excellent job. Oh, and if you could please hand out the matchmaking cards attached to this note, that would be great; I see great things for my future. Oh, and bonus, I'm ordained, so you know who to call when you get married, and Mark, I already picked out a ring, I know what she likes. That was creepier than I intended. I just love my employees and want what's best for them. Yes, I'm eccentric. But I also know people. And you two were meant to be. Report to work in two weeks; consider this an early honeymoon. Oh, and PS, you're the new bitches in charge of the Emory Games. We start next month, YAY!"

We both groaned and then realized what he'd actually done and told us.

"Wait." Olivia started pacing. "He not only knew everything but was patient enough to pull all of this off and knew he could?"

"I need to sit." I pulled out a chair and stared at her, then the note, then her. "I can't believe I'm saying this but, he's an evil genius."

"I would vote him into office," Olivia agreed, shaking her head. "I mean, we'd probably all die after giving him a big red button, but still."

"Huh." I dropped the note, then looked at her, really looked at her. "I'm thankful for him, just don't ever tell him, or I'll deny it till the day I die."

Tears filled her eyes. "Me too."

"Still hate you, though." I winked.

"Same." She laughed, then launched herself into my arms and whispered in my ear, teasing it with her tongue. "So what do you think about trying out that bathroom again and—"

I picked her up and ran.

And did exactly as Max said.

Used the next two weeks familiarizing myself with my soon-to-be wife.

And the new penthouse that had always somehow been… ours.

CONFESSIONAL *Three*

Max

"And that's why I'm the best," I said to Rick as I sat back and turned off the cameras to the penthouse after they ripped each other's clothes off. "I'm not just a hotelier; I'm a guru of love. I saw the sparks, turned them into seeds, then I fed them and watched them grow!"

Rick nodded slowly. "Wise words, wise words. Since the matchmaking part of the intern program was a wild success, do you have any plans to continue it?"

"Do pigs fly?" I laughed.

"Um, no, no, they don't."

"Well, I do, in my own private jet, so yeah, I'm gonna torture another couple. Did you see the ratings around the company? It's our best-kept secret, everyone's favorite time of year. I'm their version of Christmas, Rick, so I gotta give the people what they want. Besides, I have my eye on a few candidates." I rubbed my hands together. "I do God's work, Rick. Never forget that. In fact, tattoo it on your ass."

"Ha-ha, you're hilarious, sir, and—"

"Not a joke, Rick. Get that tattoo, or you're fired."

"Right away, sir. By the way, how's Dustin?"

"Married, two children, happy as a clam, finally got all the nerves beat out of him. The first time he yelled back at me, I shed tears real tears and gave him a promotion, proudest day of my damn life watching that little chick turn into a real bird."

"Fabulous, sir."

"Yes, yes it is. All right, now our plans for next season…Let me tell you about the next couple."

"I'm all ears."

"You will be." I smiled wickedly. "You will be."

WANT MORE RVD?

Did you enjoy Office Hate?
Then check out these other Romantic Comedies!

Bro Code

Co-Ed (Knox & Shawn's story)
Seducing Mrs. Robinson (Leo & Kora's story)
Avoiding Temptation (Slater & Tatum's story)
The Setup (Finn & Jillian's story)

The Consequence Series

The Consequence of Loving Colton (Colton & Milo's story)
The Consequence of Revenge (Max & Becca's story)
The Consequence of Seduction (Reid & Jordan's story)
The Consequence of Rejection (Jason & Maddy's story)

ACKNOWLEDGMENTS

This was a book meant for my readers as a way to say thank you. I want to make you guys laugh and am so thankful to all of you.

I love what I do but you guys make it the best!

ABOUT THE *Author*

Rachel Van Dyken is the #1 New York Times, Wall Street Journal, and USA Today bestselling author of over 90 books ranging from contemporary romance to paranormal. With over four million copies sold, she's been featured in Forbes, US Weekly, and USA Today. Her books have been translated in more than 15 countries. She was one of the first romance authors to have a Kindle in Motion book through Amazon publishing and continues to strive to be on the cutting edge of the reader experience. She keeps her home in the Pacific Northwest with her husband, adorable sons, naked cat, and two dogs. For more information about her books and upcoming events, visit www.RachelVanDykenAuthor.com.

ALSO BY
Rachel Van Dyken

Eagle Elite

Elite (Nixon & Trace's story)
Elect (Nixon & Trace's story)
Entice (Chase & Mil's story)
Elicit (Tex & Mo's story)
Bang Bang (Axel & Amy's story)
Enforce (Elite + from the boys POV)
Ember (Phoenix & Bee's story)
Elude (Sergio & Andi's story)
Empire (Sergio & Val's story)
Enrage (Dante & El's story)
Eulogy (Chase & Luciana's story)
Exposed (Dom & Tanit's story)
Envy (Vic & Renee's story)

Elite Bratva Brotherhood

RIP (Nikolai & Maya's story)
Debase (Andrei & Alice's story)

Mafia Royals Romances

Royal Bully (Asher & Claire's story)

Ruthless Princess (Serena & Junior's story

Scandalous Prince (Breaker & Violet's story)

Destructive King (Asher & Annie's story)

Mafia King (Tank & Kartini's story)

Fallen Royal (Maksim'& Izzy's story)

Broken Crown (King's story)

Rachel Van Dyken & M. Robinson

Mafia Casanova (Romeo & Eden's story)

Falling for the Villain (Juliet Sinacore's story)

Wingmen Inc.

The Matchmaker's Playbook (Ian & Blake's story)

The Matchmaker's Replacement (Lex & Gabi's story)

Bro Code

Co-Ed (Knox & Shawn's story)

Seducing Mrs. Robinson (Leo & Kora's story)

Avoiding Temptation (Slater & Tatum's story)

The Setup (Finn & Jillian's story)

Liars, Inc

Dirty Exes (Colin, Jessie & Blaire's story)

Dangerous Exes (Jessie & Isla's story)'

Cruel Summer Trilogy

Summer Heat (Marlon & Ray's story)

Summer Seduction (Marlon & Ray's story)

Summer Nights (Marlon & Ray's story)

Covet

Stealing Her (Bridge & Isobel's story)

Finding Him (Julian & Keaton's story)

The Dark Ones Series

The Dark Ones (Ethan & Genesis's story)
Untouchable Darkness (Cassius & Stephanie's story)
Dark Surrender (Alex & Hope's story)
Darkest Temptation (Mason & Serenity's story)
Darkest Sinner (Timber & Kyra's story)

Curious Liaisons

Cheater (Lucas & Avery's story)
Cheater's Regret (Thatch & Austin's story)

Red Card

Risky Play (Slade & Mackenzie's story)
Kickin' It (Matt & Parker's story)

Players Game

Fraternize (Miller, Grant and Emerson's story)
Infraction (Miller & Kinsey's story)
M.V.P. (Jax & Harley's story)

The Consequence Series

The Consequence of Loving Colton (Colton & Milo's story)
The Consequence of Revenge (Max & Becca's story)
The Consequence of Seduction (Reid & Jordan's story)
The Consequence of Rejection (Jason & Maddy's story)

The Bet Series

The Bet (Travis & Kacey's story)
The Wager (Jake & Char Lynn's story)
The Dare (Jace & Beth Lynn's story)

The Bachelors of Arizona

The Bachelor Auction (Brock & Jane's story)
The Playboy Bachelor (Bentley & Margot's story)
The Bachelor Contract (Brant & Nikki's story)

Ruin Series

Ruin (Wes Michels & Kiersten's story)
Toxic (Gabe Hyde & Saylor's story)
Fearless (Wes Michels & Kiersten's story)
Shame (Tristan & Lisa's story)

Seaside Series

Tear (Alec, Demetri & Natalee's story)
Pull (Demetri & Alyssa's story)
Shatter (Alec & Natalee's story)
Forever (Alec & Natalee's story)
Fall (Jamie Jaymeson & Pricilla's story)
Strung (Tear + from the boys POV)
Eternal (Demetri & Alyssa's story)

Seaside Pictures

Capture (Lincoln & Dani's story)
Keep (Zane & Fallon's story)
Steal (Will & Angelica's story)
All Stars Fall (Trevor & Penelope's story)
Abandon (Ty & Abigail's story)
Provoke (Braden & Piper's story)
Surrender (Andrew & Bronte's story)

Kathy Ireland & Rachel Van Dyken

Fashion Jungle

Single Titles

Office Hate (Mark & Olivia's story)
A Crown for Christmas (Fitz & Phillipa's story)
Every Girl Does It (Preston & Amanda's story)
Compromising Kessen (Christian & Kessen's story)
Divine Uprising (Athena & Adonis's story)
The Parting Gift — written with Leah Sanders (Blaine and Mara's story)

Waltzing With The Wallflower — written with Leah Sanders

Waltzing with the Wallflower (Ambrose & Cordelia)
Beguiling Bridget (Anthony & Bridget's story)
Taming Wilde (Colin & Gemma's story)

London Fairy Tales

Upon a Midnight Dream (Stefan & Rosalind's story)
Whispered Music (Dominique & Isabelle's story)
The Wolf's Pursuit (Hunter & Gwendolyn's story)
When Ash Falls (Ashton & Sofia's story)

Renwick House

The Ugly Duckling Debutante (Nicholas & Sara's story)
The Seduction of Sebastian St. James (Sebastian & Emma's story)
The Redemption of Lord Rawlings (Phillip & Abigail's story)
An Unlikely Alliance (Royce & Evelyn's story)
The Devil Duke Takes a Bride (Benedict & Katherine's story)

www.rachelvandykenauthor.com

CPSIA information can be obtained
at www.ICGtesting.com
Printed in the USA
LVHW081009150721
692794LV00016B/301